Mark caught up beside a tree a few feet away and said, "I wouldn't lean too hard on that fence."

"Why not?" I asked as I moved back from it. "I wasn't mashing it down or anything."

"That's Miss Nellie's fence, and she doesn't like anybody to come near it. If she sees you, she's liable to put some kind of spell on you."

I looked quickly over my shoulder before I laughed. "You're kidding."

"Only halfway. I doubt if Miss Nellie can really conjure up spells, but she throws a pretty mean rock for an old lady."

Books by Ann Gabhart

A Chance Hero
The Look of Eagles
The Gifting

The Gifting

ANN GABHART

CROSSWINDS

New York • Toronto
Sydney • Auckland
Manila

First publication September 1987

ISBN 0-373-98008-6

ANN GABHART was born and brought up in Kentucky, where she still lives. A real country girl, she is most happy when she is outdoors amid living and growing things. She began her very first book at the age of ten and has been writing ever since. Her three children have grown up to the sound of her typewriter clacking. Among her interests are reading, word games and basketball.

Chapter One

I sat in the back of the car, trying to act calm, while I strained for my first glimpse of the new house.

"There it is," Mama said as we rounded the curve. She slowed the car as she studied the white frame house. "It doesn't look too bad. Old and probably drafty, but at least it's big."

Cynthie stopped crying into her tissue to look up, and I couldn't control myself any longer. I rolled down my window and stuck my head out to get a better view.

"Ginny, you'll freeze us all to death," Mama said.

It was cold, but I didn't care. I had to see.

"Act your age, Ginny, for heaven's sake," Cynthie said crossly before she started crying again.

Since Cynthie had been crying for three weeks now, we didn't pay much attention to it anymore. It was as though she just had a bad cold.

Daddy had already stopped the truck in front of the house, and Charlotte and Chuck were piling out of the cab. I thought if Mama would just speed up a little, I still might beat them to the front door. She did step on the gas, and if I didn't beat them, at least my feet hit the front porch at about the same time as theirs did.

Daddy threw open the door. "Well, here it is, kids. Home."

Chuck ran in first. That was only fitting since it was the first move he could remember. Charlotte walked in after him like she was just getting home from school instead of seeing the place for the first time, but then she says she can remember moving five times. I tried to be nonchalant too, but before I knew it, I was pounding up the stairs after Chuck, crying out to the others behind us about the rooms as we ran through them for the first time.

The best discovery was the second set of narrow, curving stairs that led up to a little attic room complete with a window and pink-flowered wallpaper on the sloping walls. I held my breath until after Charlotte and Cynthie shivered and said a person would freeze this far from the heating stove. Then I could hardly keep from jumping with joy. For the first time in my life I was going to have my very own room, and that made this move the best Christmas present I could have ever gotten.

We always moved after Christmas and before New Year's. It meant we had to change schools in the middle of the year, but since Daddy was a tenant farmer, we had to move after the crops were sold and before the new crop year began.

After we had looked in every corner and closet, we started pulling the furniture off the truck and finding a place for everything in the new house. Jerry, Cathy's husband, was there to help Daddy with the heavy stuff and the unloading went twice as fast as the packing up had gone at the old house.

When all the beds were set up and boxes were piled knee-deep in the downstairs rooms, I began edging toward the front door.

"Mom, Ginny's trying to sneak off," Charlotte said.

Mama looked up from her circle of boxes. She was opening them one by one and peeking inside before she sent them off to the proper rooms.

"I just want to look around outside," I said.

"I guess you're going out to look at the cows," Cynthie stopped sniffling long enough to say.

"I like cows," I said.

"You just don't like unpacking," Charlotte said.

"Leave her alone," Cathy spoke up from her chair by the stove. She had her hands spread out on her swollen belly as though she needed to hold the baby inside. "She helped Mom pack while you two were out saying goodbye to the scenery back at the other house. So I guess she's got a right to go and check out the new scenery first."

Cynthie started crying louder than before, and Charlotte got a dreamy look on her face. "I hope there're some cute guys around here," Charlotte said. "That's my kind of scenery."

I kept my eyes on Mama while they talked, and after a minute she just said, "Wear your coat, Ginny. It's winter, don't forget."

I grabbed my coat and was out on the porch before anybody could say anything else. I looked over my shoulder, glad that I didn't see Chuck. I wanted to make this first exploration by myself, and if Chuck saw me, he'd have to tag along.

As I headed across the field, I was glad to be free of the family and most of all the sisters. Having three older sisters wasn't the easiest thing in the world, especially since I was so different from the rest.

They had brown hair. Mine was somewhere between red and blond. They had green eyes. I had blue. They were short with all the right measurements, and I was tall and close to skinny though I was beginning to stretch out in a few of the right places now that I was thirteen.

Still, I wasn't just different in the way I looked. All their names started with a *C*—Cathy, Cynthia, Charlotte. Even Chuck's name started with a *C*. Thinking about my name, Virginia, made me wonder sometimes if I was adopted.

The sisters had all had boyfriends by the time they were thirteen, and I never knew how to talk to boys, at least not like that. Boys made good buddies to trade comic books with or to shoot a few hoops with, but I wasn't sure about this holding hands and kissing stuff.

I looked down at my hands. I couldn't have held hands with anybody even if I had wanted to. Not with those awful warts. I had three warts on the end of one finger and one especially ugly, seedy thing sitting up on my middle knuckle where everybody could see it, whether I held hands or not. Most of the time I tried to keep my hands out of sight in my pockets or behind my back.

The warts were just another way I was different. None of the sisters had ever had even one tiny little wart, much less a whole bumper crop like me.

When I saw the cows, I forgot about my warts. I really did like cows. The sisters thought that was not only dumb, but a little crazy as well, and they were always teasing me about it.

The new cows, black and white holsteins, turned their heads toward me but kept chewing their cuds while their breath came out of their noses in puffs of white steam in the cool air. Out of habit I stopped and counted them, though I didn't know how many there were supposed to be. One old cow got to her feet, but even she wasn't worried enough to move away when I walked closer.

Once through the cows, I stood still and looked around to decide which way to go next. Behind me I heard Chuck come out in the yard and yell for me. I walked faster toward a fence and a stand of trees.

It didn't really matter which direction I chose today. I'd get to explore all the directions sooner or later while we were at the Shelley farm. There was even some hope that we wouldn't have to move again, at least not until Daddy got enough saved up to buy our own place since this farm was owned by a doctor and he didn't spare any expense on the stock and the land. We had every chance of making money here.

The tree house caught my eye as I climbed over the fence. The kind of tree house I'd always dreamed of building, it was perched comfortably on two sturdy oak limbs and was more than just a plank to sit on. It had a roof, walls, and even a couple of square windows.

I had my foot on the first step nailed on the tree trunk when up above, a foot touched the top step. I jerked back away from the tree like it had scorched me.

The foot became a leg, then two legs, and finally arms and a head as the boy stretched down from the bottom step to the top.

"Hi," he said as he jumped to the ground. "I didn't aim to scare you."

"You could have said something to let me know you were up there," I said. Then I looked at the fence. "But I guess maybe I'm trespassing so I should be the one to say I'm sorry."

He smiled. "Neither one of us is trespassing. I guess we'll sort of be sharing these woods and fields for a while. I'm Mark Shelley."

He was taller than I was with smoky blue eyes and dark hair that lapped over his forehead. All in all he was a pretty nice-looking boy, and I thought Cynthie and Charlotte might not mind seeing this bit of scenery even if he was more my age than theirs.

"Oh, your father must be Dr. Shelley."

"Yeah. Do you want to come up and see the tree house? I haven't used it much lately."

"It's a little cold today, isn't it? To be sitting in a tree house, I mean."

His face reddened a little. Then he smiled again. "Well, you get a pretty good view of things from up there."

"You were spying on us."

"Sort of." He looked off at our new house across the field. "Dad said there were kids, and I was curious."

"There are kids all right. Lots of kids."

"Are you all one family?"

"All one family. There are five of us in all, but Cathy is married now. I guess we looked like a herd moving in."

"I wish I had brothers and sisters."

"You might not wish that if you did." I looked from him to the tree house. "Can you really see what's going on over at the house?"

"Sure. Come on up and see for yourself."

The tree house was even nicer than I had imagined, with shelves, a trunk that doubled as a chair, and a small table. When we sat on the floor, the window was eye level, and our new house was framed in the open space.

Without a word, he handed me a pair of binoculars. They brought Chuck close enough that I could see the picture of Spiderman on his sweat shirt.

"This isn't a tree house. It's a sentry post," I said.

"You could say that. But this was the only really good tree for a tree house when I built it when I was ten."

"You built this when you were ten?" I stared at the neatly fitted boards. There were hardly any cracks or bent nails.

"Mr. Wilson helped me. He was our tenant before Mr. Johnson who just moved. But you don't have to look at the house. You can look this way out over the other trees. I used to see a deer every once in a while."

"You don't any more?"

"I haven't been out here for a while."

"You just came out to watch us move in."

Mark ducked his head and then looked up with a grin. "I guess it wasn't too nice a thing to do, but I wasn't hurting anybody. I just wanted to see how old you were and everything."

"You want to come over and meet everybody, or do you just want me to point them out from here when they poke their heads outside?"

"It might be nice to know your names. You haven't even told me yours yet."

"I haven't, have I?" I put the binoculars back to my eyes and stared through them at the house. "Maybe I'll let you guess."

He scooted back to lean against the tree trunk. "I know your last name's Todd. I guess I could call you that."

"Todd? That sounds like a boy's first name," I said, suddenly very conscious that I wasn't a boy.

"Then how about Toad?"

All my warts throbbed to life. The kids back at the old school had sometimes called me that. Toad.

Slinging the binoculars at him, I skinned through the hole in the floor, missed the last three steps, and landed on my bottom side. The boy stuck his head out the entrance hole. "Are you hurt?"

"No." I scrambled to my feet and then tried to move away from the tree house in a dignified manner the way one of the sisters might have.

Mark jumped down to the ground as light as a cat and caught up with me. "Look, I didn't mean to make you mad. I was just trying to get you to tell me your name. Toad sounds sort of like Todd."

"Yeah, sure. I guess you didn't even think about me having warts like a toad frog." I waved my hand in front of his face. The big, ugly wart was bleeding.

"I didn't know you had warts."

I couldn't tell if he was lying or not, but I decided it didn't matter. I should have just told him my name to begin with. He'd told me his. "My name's Ginny, short for Virginia which I guess is almost as bad as Toad."

"There's nothing wrong with your name," Mark said. "Or with having warts. My dad says most warts are sort of like a virus. They come and go like colds."

"Mine don't seem to want to go," I said and put my hand behind my back. "Do you want to go back to the house with me and meet the rest of the family?"

"Do you have to go back right now?"

"I probably should. The sisters will be griping, but I don't have to go back unless somebody hollers for me."

"Somebody was hollering for you a while ago."

I looked around at him. "That's right. Chuck was, so you knew my name all along. Maybe I should get mad again."

Mark looked over at me sideways and grinned a little. "I thought maybe you had a dog named Ginny."

Without thinking I gave his shoulder a shove and then took off running through the woods. As I dodged trees and fallen branches and groundhog holes, staying just one step in front of him, I thought the sisters wouldn't be caught dead running through the woods like a wild Indian. Especially with a cute guy like Mark around to see them.

Another fence stopped me, and I leaned against it while I caught my breath. I felt great. Running always made me feel that way.

Mark caught up with me, but he didn't lean against the woven wire fence. He sank down beside a tree a few feet away and said, "I wouldn't lean too hard on that fence."

"Why not?" I asked as I moved back away from it. "I wasn't mashing it down or anything."

"That's Miss Nellie's fence, and she doesn't like anybody touching it. If she sees you, she's liable to put some kind of spell on you."

I looked quickly over my shoulder before I laughed. "You're kidding."

"Only halfway. I doubt if Miss Nellie can really conjure up spells, but she throws a pretty mean rock for an old lady."

"But I don't see anybody."

The trees on the other side of the fence were thicker than on this side. Their branches were touching up high and down below bushes and dead weeds made the going look rough.

"She might see you, though." Mark was staring at the trees. "It is sort of spooky looking when you think about it."

The more he talked the darker the shadows under the cedars and other trees became. "Is some kind of ghost going to pop out at me next?" My laugh sounded a little shaky.

"No ghosts unless little Annie is in there haunting the place."

"Little Annie?"

"A little girl they say Miss Nellie killed. But Dad says it's just a lot of tales or gossip." Mark set up and stared at the trees. "If you look right through there you can see Miss Nellie's house."

I looked where he pointed, and I could see something white through the trees. It looked more like the ghost of a house, if houses could have ghosts, and a funny little chill climbed up my backbone. At the same time that I wanted to run away, I had the urge to sneak through the woods till I was close enough to see what the house really looked like.

"Tell me more about Miss Nellie," I said.

"There's not much to tell. She's just an old lady who doesn't like people bothering her."

"Does she live there all by herself?"

"All alone except for the ghosts."

"You just said there weren't any ghosts."

"There's not. I just like to watch you shiver." Mark grinned.

I smiled, too.

"Actually you probably have more ghosts in the house you just moved into," Mark said. "It's had a lot of people living in it. Miss Nellie's grandfather built her house and nobody but Springwoods have ever lived there and not many of them."

"Springwood. That's the name of the town."

"Miss Nellie's grandfather was a founding father."

"How old is she?"

"Nobody's sure. Dad says she has to be in her eighties and that she really shouldn't be living out here all by herself."

"That must be weird. Living in the same place all your life."

"How many places have you lived?" Mark asked.

"Four, but I can only remember three and now here."

"Talk about weird. That sounds really weird to me."

I shrugged and got up. "It's not so bad. I sort of like moving. You get to meet lots of people."

"But don't you hate leaving behind all your old friends?"

"Mama says you can't worry about what you're leaving behind. That you have to think about all the good things you're moving to. In this case the house is twice as nice even if it has a dozen ghosts. I'm even going to get my own room."

"Let me guess. The one up in the attic."

"I guess you know the house better than I do."

"I always go look it over after somebody moves to see if they left anything behind."

"Ever find anything interesting?"

"A quarter once. A pocketknife another time, but Dad made me give that back."

"Well, I'll leave you something exciting when we move."

"Don't talk about moving," Mark said. "You just moved in, and I think you all are going to be lots more fun than the last tenants we had."

"You mean more fun to spy on?"

"I did used to spy on Mr. and Mrs. Johnson. They did everything at the same time. You could have set your clock by when they ate and fed their cat and went to bed. Boring."

"Maybe we'll be more interesting."

"I'm too old for all that nonsense now. Spying and all. If I want to know what you're doing, I'll just come over and see."

"Sure. That's why you were watching us through the binoculars today."

"Dad told me not to go over and bother you till you got settled in, and I wanted to see if there was a boy who might play basketball with me. I've got a goal over at the house."

"Maybe a girl will do. I played on the girls' team back in Overton."

"No kidding?" Mark said. "I play for the team here."

Through the trees came the echo of my name. For a minute the chill hit my backbone again as I looked over my shoulder at the trees closing in around Miss Nellie's almost invisible house. But the cry was coming from the other direction.

"Somebody must be hollering for you," Mark said. "I'd have never believed we could have heard it way over here."

"You don't know Charlotte. She could call the cows home from the next county."

I started off through the woods. "Why don't you come on home with me, and I'll introduce you to everybody proper like?"

"Why not?" Mark said. "Dad wouldn't want me to be unfriendly."

A nice little warm feeling tickled my insides. I couldn't wait to see the sisters' faces when I showed up on the doorstep with Mark.

Chapter Two

Before the week was out all the boxes were unpacked or shoved away out of sight. The big old house already seemed like home, and though my attic room proved to be just as drafty and cold as the sisters had predicted, I loved it.

I especially liked the little staircase with the door at the bottom. When I went up those narrow steps, I felt I was climbing away from the world. Sitting by the window, wrapped in a blanket with my breath hanging like white smoke in the air, I could lose myself in a book and never once have to look up to answer a question.

Charlotte called me a recluse like old Miss Nellie.

Chuck looked up from his TV show to ask Mom, "What's a recluse?" He had that funny worried frown that made the sisters laugh.

"Someone who lives by himself and doesn't want other people around. Sort of like a hermit," Mom said, looking up from peeling potatoes.

"Then Ginny can't be a recluse." Chuck stumbled over the word.

"That's for sure. Not with a family like this." I ruffled his hair a little and plopped down beside him in front of the television. "What are you watching?"

"Spiderman." His eyes locked back on the screen.

Cynthie looked around at me from her spot by the window. Cynthie had stopped crying. The second day we went to school, she'd come home with a dreamy look that meant a new love was on the horizon, and now she liked to sit close to the window just in case he happened to drive by on the road out front. She lost her dreamy look long enough to say, "Guess who's coming, Ginny?"

"Mark," I said without moving from my spot on the floor.

"How'd you guess, Ginny?" Charlotte said in a singsong voice. "Were you expecting him?"

Cynthie chimed in again. "No sir, Ginny can't be a recluse. Not with a boyfriend, and Ginny has a boyfriend."

I took a deep breath and concentrated on Spiderman throwing his web over the bad guys.

"Hush, girls," Mama said. Then when we heard him step up on the porch, she looked at me. "Go let him in, Ginny."

But Chuck was up ahead of me, making a mad dash behind the stove to reach the door first.

"Don't run behind the stove, Chuck," Mama said as he skimmed past the stovepipe. "You're going to get burned."

Chuck yanked open the door before Mark could knock. "Hi, Chuck," Mark said. "Do you and Ginny want to go sleigh riding? The snow's just right."

"Come on in, Mark, and warm up while Ginny gets her things on," Charlotte called and then nudged me hard with her toe.

"I can't. I've got snow all over my boots," Mark said.

"The floor's been wet before. Besides, you're letting all our heat out," Mama said, and Chuck pulled Mark inside.

Chuck, who thought Mark was the greatest thing since Saturday morning cartoons, would have followed Mark around like a little puppy dog if Mama and Daddy had let him. The sisters liked Mark too, and he even said he liked them. Of course they were nice to him. It was only me they teased.

It was still snowing as we walked toward what Mark said was the best hill for miles around.

"Dad says we may get six inches," Mark said. "We won't have to go to school for a week at least. It'll take them that long to clear the county roads for the school buses."

"And we can go sleigh riding every day," Chuck said.

"Sure, kid," Mark said. "If it doesn't get too cold."

"It's cold enough today," I said, reaching over to pull Chuck's sock hat down. "You'd better keep your ears covered or you'll have an earache and then Mama won't let you go outside anymore."

Chuck yanked his hat down over his head until his eyes were barely showing. He sat down on the sled and said, "Now I can't see. You'll have to pull me the rest of the way."

"I'll pull you, kid," Mark said.

"You're carrying this 'I'd like to have a little brother' thing a little far, don't you think?" I said as I watched him begin pulling the sled.

"Chuck's not heavy."

"No, he's your brother, right?" I shook my head at Mark. "How much farther is this wonderful hill?"

"It's over between Miss Nellie's and the store. Not far. There's Miss Nellie's fence up ahead."

As soon as we passed the corner post, the trees grew thicker and denser. Even the snow seemed heavier in the gray air as the flakes settled on the cedar branches until they drooped to the ground under the load. I looked up through the trees as I did every time we passed Miss Nellie's place, but though her house was easier to see from here than from the line fence behind our house, today the snow hid it from sight.

Chuck got off the sled and came to walk close beside me. None of us had seen Miss Nellie yet, though Mark said she walked to the store at least once a week.

But we'd heard enough stories so that it was hard not to walk a little faster than normal when we went by her place on the way to the store. Chuck cried if I didn't let him keep touching me till we were past her fence line.

Now Chuck looked up through the trees where it looked like no person had set foot for years and said, "She's a recluse."

"A reclu-oo-ooze." Mark made his voice sound as spooky as possible.

"Hush, both of you. She's probably just an old lady who doesn't like all the noise people are always making," I said.

"Especially kids' noise. She turns little kids into trees," Mark said. He reached up, grabbed a cedar branch, and shook the snow down on us.

Shrieking, Chuck took off in a run. Mark and I ran after him and didn't stop till we got to the hill the other side of Miss Nellie's place where some other kids were already making paths up and down the hill with their sleds.

The snow was just right for sledding, and it wasn't long till even Chuck quit looking over at the trees behind us to make sure Miss Nellie wasn't sneaking up on him.

I was at the bottom of the hill trying to shake the snow out of my gloves from my latest crash landing when I heard Mark yelling up on top of the hill. "Watch out, Chuck."

I looked around in time to see Chuck barreling straight toward someone making his way along through the field toward the road. The man plodded through the snow without looking to either side. At the same time, Chuck had his sock hat pulled down over his eyes until he could barely see straight in front of him, and he was laughing with the thrill of the fast trip down the hill.

I dropped my gloves and ran toward the man. "Look out," I yelled, but he didn't even look up.

At the last second Chuck saw the man in his path and ditched the sled, but the sled bounced away from Chuck and banged against the man's legs. He went down hard in the snow.

"Are you all right?" I asked the man as I grabbed his arm to help him up.

As he sat up, his hat fell off and underneath was long gray hair wrapped tightly in a bun. The old woman slapped my hand away and began probing her legs and arms.

The other kids were making a circle around us, but they stayed well back. I waited till she had finished feeling all her bones before I asked, "Do you think anything's broken?"

"No," she said crossly. "Well, don't just stand there like a knot on a log. Help me up."

I took hold under her arm and lifted her up. She was surprisingly light in spite of her bulky look. "My little brother didn't mean to knock you down."

"Your little brother, eh. Which one?" She turned and peered at the circle of kids. Other kids were running down from the top of the hill, Mark among them.

Chuck tried to sink back out of sight, but I grabbed him and pulled him forward. "Tell the lady you're sorry."

Chuck managed to mumble something close to an apology, but the old lady's frown didn't soften. "You'd be wise to learn to watch where you're going, young man," she said.

"Yes, ma'am," he said. He pulled away from me and edged back behind the other kids.

Mark pushed through them. "Are you okay, Miss Nellie? Do you want me to call my father?"

"Now why would I want you to do that? I just took a little spill in the snow. From the looks of you, I'd say you'd taken several spills." Her eyes narrowed on him, and her frown grew fiercer. "And I won't be needing none of young Dr. Joseph's poking or prodding. He'd be trying to ship me off to an old folks' home some- where."

She stared around the circle at us, and it was so quiet we could almost hear the snowflakes hitting our caps. "Well, get my hat, one of you," she said.

I snatched it up and handed it to her. It was a man's cap with furry ear muffs.

Taking it from me without any kind of thank-you, she shoved it back on her head and then adjusted her wool muffler up over the back of her neck. "Don't stand there gawking. Get on about your business," she said.

The other kids scattered back up the hill. Chuck ran away the fastest. But Mark and I waited to make sure she was really all right. I guess we felt more responsible than the others since he was my little brother using Mark's sled.

All of a sudden she reached out and grabbed my hand. I jumped and tried to pull away, but her bony grasp was strong as a hawk's.

"How many have you got?" she asked.

"How many what?" I stammered.

"Warts." She pulled my hand up close to her eyes. "I'll take them off if you don't want them."

I checked to see if maybe she was pulling a knife out of her pocket with her other hand. "How?" I asked.

"Never mind that. If you don't want them, just tell me how many you've got and they'll be gone in two weeks."

I didn't think I'd ever get my hand back if I didn't tell her what she wanted to know. "Eleven, I think," I said. "Maybe twelve."

"I suppose that's close enough, but it's better to be exact." She dropped my hand and started on toward the store. She moved slowly, setting her feet down firmly in the snow, one at a time like old cows did in the slick mud around a pond.

Even after I'd found my gloves, had put them back on and was at the top of the hill ready for another slide down, I could feel the grip of her fingers on my hand.

When she came back out of the store, Mark and I watched as she made her way back down the road and then across the field toward her land. "I should have called my dad," Mark said. "She might have broken something."

"She said she was all right." I looked around for Chuck. I didn't want a repeat performance, but I needn't have worried. Chuck stayed at the top of the hill until Miss Nellie disappeared into the woods on her land. Then he waited another five minutes before he dared go down the hill again.

The day we went back to school I glanced down at my hands in math class and noticed the big, ugly wart on my knuckle didn't look quite as big as before. I stared at my hand until the bell rang.

As the days passed, my eyes seemed to be pulled to my hand every few minutes. I could only find six warts left now, and the others were fading fast. The big one was hardly noticeable by the end of ten days and hadn't bled for days.

Late one afternoon when Chuck and I were over at Mark's house shooting baskets, I dared to ask Mark, "Do you think Miss Nellie has special powers or anything?"

"Powers? What do you mean?" Mark moved around me to sink the basketball in the hoop.

"My warts are almost gone."

Letting the ball bounce away from the goal, Mark came over and grabbed my hand. "How about that? They are. I'd heard people say she could make warts go away, but I never believed it."

"Do you now?" I asked. "I mean how could she make my warts go away just by looking at them and asking me how many I had?"

Chuck pushed in between us to look at my hand and then up at me with his eyes wide and shiny. "The kids at school say she's a witch."

Mark laughed. "And I guess you believe them."

"I don't know," Chuck said.

"If she'd been a witch she'd have turned you into a tree stump or something that day you ran into her on the sledding hill," Mark said.

Chuck's eyes got even wider. "Do you think she could?"

"Don't be silly, Chuck. Mark's just teasing you."

"But she took your warts off," Chuck said.

"I don't know whether she did or not," I said.

"You think she did or you wouldn't have been asking Mark about it."

"Well, even if she did, it wouldn't mean she was a witch." I pulled my hand away from Mark.

"No, she's a reclu-oo-ooze, remember, kid?" Mark said.

He was going after the ball when his father pulled in the drive. "I tell you what," Mark said. "We'll ask Dad what he thinks."

"Yeah, he ought to know. He's a doctor," Chuck said.

Dr. Shelley solemnly looked at my hand. He had dark hair and eyebrows and always looked so serious and rushed that I got tongue-tied every time I tried to say hello to him. So now I just held out my hand without a word.

"What do you think, Dad? I mean Ginny had this horrible wart right there, and now it's almost gone."

Mark poked his finger down on what remained of the wart on my knuckle.

"Then I think she's probably glad it went away. Warts are like that. They stay a while, and then one day they just disappear." Dr. Shelley gave my hand a pat and then dropped it. He smiled at us in an absent-minded way before heading for the house.

Mark stopped him. "But Dad, do you think Miss Nellie did it?"

Dr. Shelley's smile was real now as he looked at us. "Oh, so that's what this is all about. You think Miss Nellie made your warts go away."

Since he was staring straight at me, I had to answer. "I don't know. It's just that she said they'd be gone in two weeks, and it's been almost two weeks now."

When he laughed, he sounded like Mark. "All those stories about her being a witch have got you a little nervous, have they?"

"Come on, Dad," Mark said. "Stop making fun of us."

Dr. Shelley's smile was gentler now, and I decided he might not be such a bad doctor to call on when you were sick, after all. "I'm not making fun of you." He looked at me. "I don't know whether Miss Nellie made your warts go away or not, Ginny, but if you're asking my professional opinion, I'd say she didn't and that it was simply a coincidence of timing. They were going to go away some time anyway. But one thing for sure, you don't have to worry about Miss Nellie doing you any harm."

"But what about little Annie?" Chuck asked.

Dr. Shelley's smile disappeared. "What do you know about her?"

Chuck edged over close to me. "Rachel—she's in my class at school—she said that Miss Nellie killed her and that she might kill other kids who were dumb enough to bother her."

Dr. Shelley sighed. "Poor little Annie. Some people just won't forget. But what you have to remember, Chuck, is that stories have a way of getting exaggerated completely out of reason when they're told over and over, and this story has been told for close to twenty-five years now. Miss Nellie won't hurt you, but she doesn't like people trespassing on her property. So stay on our side of the fence."

Chuck nodded.

"But what about the little girl called Annie?" I asked. Mark kicked me, but I ignored him. "What happened to her?"

Dr. Shelley's frown was fierce. "It's a long story," he said. "One that's better forgotten."

"I'm sorry," I stammered. "I was just curious."

"Curiosity can be a bad thing. But if you want to know the truth, we were all a little to blame for the child's death." He turned and disappeared into the house.

Mark walked back across the fields with us as far as the tree house. Since Chuck couldn't go past the tree house without crawling up in it to have a look at everything, we stopped under the tree while he climbed up, even though it was almost dark.

"I'm sorry about Dad," Mark said. "But I tried to warn you."

"I guess I shouldn't have been so nosy. Mama says I'm always asking questions I shouldn't."

"Little Annie is sort of a taboo subject around our house."

"Then you don't know what happened to her, either." I turned to stare in the direction of Miss Nellie's house, but I couldn't even see her trees from here.

"Not really. I've just heard the old stories like the one Chuck heard, but nothing that could be the truth. Dad did tell me once that Miss Nellie used to be sort of a country doctor. Before there was a real doctor here, people would go to her, and she'd give them herbs and things. Dad said it was harmless, but useless too."

"You think that has anything to do with the story about little Annie?"

"I don't know. I just know if you're around my house, it's safer not to ask."

Chuck jumped off the last step, down beside us. "You could always ask Miss Nellie," he said.

"Yeah, sure," I said with a grin at him. "First thing in the morning, and you can go with me."

Chuck shivered and then was off over the fence running for the barn. Waving at Mark, I followed Chuck. Mark and I couldn't talk. We were both laughing too hard.

Chapter Three

When I woke early a few days later to see a blanket of new snow out my window, I knew there wouldn't be any school, but I didn't scoot back under the covers. The early morning was the best time to explore in the new snow and the best time to make my escape from the house without Chuck. The sun was just coming up when I let myself out the back door.

Dad already had the cows in the barn. I heard the chug of the milkers as I went by, but I didn't stop to help him.

Once away from the barn and in the woods, the snow smoothed out clean and unspoiled again. My tracks trailing off behind me were the only signs of life, and looking back, I wished I could erase those marks in the snow. Almost in answer to my wish a wind blew through the trees, shaking snow down on me and sweeping away my footprints.

At Miss Nellie's fence, I stopped and pulled off my glove. Only smooth skin met my eyes. The warts were gone without a trace just as my footprints were.

I looked toward Miss Nellie's house, but it was hard to tell the white of her house from the white of the snow nestled in the cedar branches.

I stared down at my hand again. Then I pulled my glove back on and before I could think about it any more, climbed the fence.

The woods changed once I was on the other side of the fence. The trees were thicker, and I kept brushing against the low-hanging cedars and knocking loose their loads of snow. The woods were almost eerily silent and dim in spite of the spots of sunshine that shoved down through the branches here and there. Even the wind seemed to have to sneak down below the trees to blow.

There was no cleared area around the house. No yard. The trees grew right up to the large front porch, the limbs brushing against the sides of the house. I stopped beside a large oak tree, and half-concealed behind it, I watched the house.

I stood there staring at Miss Nellie's house for so long that when I looked back, my tracks were only vague dips in the snow. If I went on up to that house and disappeared inside it never to be seen again, no one would ever know what had happened to me. Just like little Annie.

"You're getting as bad as Chuck," I whispered to myself with a little laugh. "Nothing is going to happen to you. You're going to go up there, knock on her door, and thank her for taking away your warts. That's all."

Still, in spite of the pep talk, my feet were heavy as I moved away from the tree toward the house. Miss Nellie was different. Everybody said that, and I knew it was true because I had seen her myself. She had to be different to live here by herself in a house that the trees seemed to be holding prisoner.

I stopped again, but then I told myself I was different, too. Different from the sisters. But at least the warts that had been one of my ways of being different were gone, and I had Miss Nellie to thank for that, no matter what Mark's father had said.

The porch had been swept clean of snow. I went across it and knocked timidly on the old-fashioned screen door, making it jar against its frame. Then I waited. If she didn't open the door in three minutes, I'd go back through the woods and home. I began counting slowly.

I was only up to thirty when the door creaked open. "So you got the nerve to come on up to the door, did you?" the old lady asked.

I just stared at her. Without her covering of coats and hats and scarves, she looked odder than ever, just a frail shadow of a woman in men's corduroy pants and a faded green flannel shirt.

She squinted at me. "I've been watching you, and me and Midnight didn't think you'd get up the nerve, but Sunlight did. Sunlight's always ready to give you kids the benefit of the doubt.''

I swallowed hard and tried to think of the words I'd come to say, but my mind was blank.

She opened the door a bit wider. ''Well, come on in,'' she said. ''That is what you wanted to do, wasn't it?''

Finally I found my voice. ''I just came to thank you for taking off my warts.'' I groped at my glove to pull it off.

''You don't have to show me. I know they're gone. I said they would be, didn't I?''

I nodded and stood there with my glove half on and half off.

She reached out, took hold of my arm, and pulled me through the door. ''It's a long way back through the snow to your house. You'd better warm up before you go.''

I looked down at my boots. ''I'll get snow all over your floor.''

''Then stand on one of the papers and take your boots off, for heaven's sake.''

When my eyes adjusted to the dimness of the room after the bright sun on the snow outside, I could see the newspapers scattered around the room. A pair of work boots were drying out on one behind the stove. A rumpled paper was at the foot of a rocking chair. A black cat lay on another newspaper which covered a stool close to the rocking chair. Then in the corner a thick layer of papers was spread out below a hawk who sat calmly eyeing me from his perch.

As I stepped over on one of the papers just inside the door and began unfastening my boots, a yellow-striped cat came over to rub up against my legs. I ran my hand down his back. He didn't seem to mind that my fingers were shaky as he stuck his head into my palm and purred.

"That's Sunlight's way of saying he told us so. Of course me and Midnight are usually right. Most of the kids stop about Richard out there, and then after they think about it for a while, they tear a branch off of one of the little trees and run off with it like they've captured some kind of trophy."

"He's a pretty cat," I said. My eyes were pulled to the hawk again who was still watching me coldly.

"Pretty enough," Miss Nellie said.

"I really didn't aim to come in and bother you, Miss Nellie," I said as I slipped off my boots.

"My name's not Nellie," she said crossly.

I looked up at her.

"Oh, don't look so addled. I know that's what the folks all call me, but it doesn't make Nellie my name. Nellie is a mule's name."

"What is your name then?"

"Eleanore. Eleanore Barton Springwood. The Eleanore was after my grandmother and the Barton after my mother."

"It's a pretty name."

"Do you think everything's pretty, child?" she said with some annoyance. "So now you know my name, what's yours? I know you're one of the Todd children."

"Ginny," I said.

"That sounds like a donkey. A mule and donkey." She laughed and sat down in the wooden rocking chair. The black cat slowly raised his head to look at her. "Did you hear that, Midnight? A mule and a donkey."

I stepped out of my boots and stared down at my big toe working its way through a hole in my sock. I said, "My whole name is Virginia Mae Todd."

"Virginia. I went to school with a girl named Virginia."

"That was my grandmother's name."

"Then we're still a pair. Both named after our grandmothers." She rocked back and forth a few times while Sunlight kept rubbing first one way and then the other against my legs. "Come closer to the stove. You can't warm up way back there."

As I moved to the stove, the hawk lifted his wings away from his body and shook a little before dropping them down again.

"That's Hawk," the old lady said. "And don't say he's pretty. He'd be insulted."

I stared at the bird. "How about grand?"

"Better," the old lady said. "But it's hard to describe a wild creature as anything but wild, and really wild is the best word when you think about it. Wild."

"If he's wild, why is he in the house?"

"He's just resting here for a spell. Somebody shot one of his wings, but it's about healed now. He'll be able to fend for himself again soon." She laughed. "Midnight will be glad. He and Hawk have been eyeing each other for weeks now. I don't know whether Midnight is worried about Hawk eating him or if he wants to eat Hawk.''

She motioned to the black cat. "This, by the way, is Midnight, if you hadn't guessed.''

I leaned over to touch the black cat's head, but he sprang up, arched his back, and spat at me. I jerked my hand back.

"Midnight would like to be wild,'' Miss Nellie said. Then she shivered a little before she added, ''Since you're standing up, Virginia, would you be kind enough to throw another chunk of wood in the stove? My rheumatism has got my knees in knots this morning.''

I took the last piece of wood out of the woodbox just inside the door and carefully put it in the stove. Then as the fire roared to new life, I began to feel too warm with my coat on, but I didn't take it off.

Behind me on the mantel, an ancient pendulum clock steadily stroked away the seconds. Sunlight still purred as he wound his way around my legs while the other cat had turned his back to me and was staring at the hawk. Though the rocker creaked as it moved back and forth, the old lady's eyes were shut, and I thought she might have fallen asleep. I didn't know how to leave without waking her up.

Her hands and face were pale with the blue veins barely beneath the surface of her skin. I tried to see her breathing so that I could tell if she was really asleep, but her shirt was so large and bulky that I couldn't even see her chest move at all.

What if she were dead? I swallowed hard and watched her eyelids for a twitch of movement. When I could stand it no longer, I said, "Miss Eleanore?"

"I'm not asleep." She opened her eyes slowly. "Or dead. Don't look so alarmed."

"I'd better be getting back home." I began edging toward my boots. "I didn't tell anybody where I was going."

"She is a brave youngster, dearies." Miss Eleanore leaned forward in her chair and stared at me. "Weren't you afraid I'd turn you into a tree?"

"A tree?"

"Isn't that what the children say? That I'm a witch who turns trespassers into trees."

"I don't know what the other kids say, but I don't think you're going to turn me into a tree."

"How else do you suppose there got to be so many trees around my house?"

"They grew here the same as anywhere else."

She laughed. "You're young to be so sensible, Virginia Mae Todd. Yet you did believe I took your warts away."

"You said they'd be gone in two weeks and they were. How did you do it?" I looked up from pulling on my boots. "Take the warts away, I mean."

"It's a secret passed down to me from my grandfather who was the seventh son of a seventh son. One of several secrets and the least important one. Warts take very little power."

I stared at her for a minute before I said, "You're beginning to sound more like a witch now."

Miss Eleanore smiled. "Midnight will be pleased. He's always wanted to be a witch's cat. After all, he's the right color." She stopped smiling. "I haven't scared you, have I?"

"No. Just made me curious, but I've been told that curiosity..."

"Killed the cat. Well, you're not a cat." She leaned back and shut her eyes again. "You'll forgive me if I don't see you to the door, but this snow has tired out my bones."

The snow lay deep on her wood stack. Looking at it, I hesitated. Then before I had time to wonder if I should or shouldn't, I brushed the snow off the wood and picked up an arm-load. I didn't knock but just pushed through the door and dropped the wood in the box.

Miss Eleanore opened her eyes and frowned at me, but I was back out the door before she could say anything. It took me eight trips to fill up the box.

Then instead of thanking me, she said, "I'm not so feeble, I can't pack in my own wood."

"I just wanted to do something for you after you'd done something for me."

The look on her face softened the barest bit.

"I'd like to come back and see you again sometime," I said. The words surprised me almost as much as they did her.

After staring at me for a long moment, she said, "Sunlight would like that. Just don't go telling anybody. I wouldn't want my reputation for turning folks into trees to be spoiled. I'd be having people in and out of here all the time. It's bad enough that young Dr. Joseph keeps coming around every month trying to cart me off to an old folks' home. Says it'd ease his mind to know I was some place where people could take care of me. As if I wasn't able to take care of myself."

"I won't tell anybody," I promised.

"Good. Then tell Richard to be expecting you when you go back through the field."

The trees didn't seem so unfriendly as I walked back through them. Actually it was a beautiful woods, thick and quiet, and I would have liked to explore more of it. But I knew I'd better get back to the house. Mom and Dad would be back from the barn by now, and somebody might miss me.

I was back on our side of the fence before I realized that I hadn't asked Miss Eleanore who Richard was.

Chapter Four

"Where have you been, Ginny?" Charlotte asked when I came into the kitchen.

"I took a walk," I said.

"You had a phone call," Charlotte said.

"From a boy," Cynthie added.

Sometimes I thought they must rehearse. I sighed. "What did Mark want?"

"So you think it was Mark, do you?" Charlotte said. "Who'd have ever thought Ginny would get the most calls from boys after we moved."

"I guess she's blossoming at last," Cynthie said.

"Oh, why don't you both shut up?" I said. "Mark's just a friend."

"We should all have friends like that," Cynthie said and poked Charlotte's shoulder.

Charlotte rolled her eyes. "Nice, good-looking, and with those gorgeous blue eyes."

"It's a shame he's not a little older so you two could fight over him," I said.

"Come on, Ginny. Don't get mad," Cynthie said.

"Nobody with a boyfriend like Mark has any right to get mad," Charlotte chimed in.

"He's not my boyfriend." My face was beginning to burn.

"You just said he was a friend," Charlotte said.

"And he's certainly a boy," Cynthie added. "So he has to be a boy friend."

"That's enough," Mama said quietly from the sink. She always knew when I was ready to start hitting. "Get something to eat, Ginny, and then you and Chuck can go help your father get up wood."

I liked going with Daddy to get wood. That day as I rode in the trailer back through the trees, I wondered who got up Miss Eleanore's wood. I couldn't imagine her handling a chain saw or an axe, but then I had a hard time imagining her carrying the wood in to fill the woodbox. She had looked so frail.

Chuck and I stayed well back out of the way while Dad felled the big ash tree. It shuddered and went down with a crash, sending up a spray of snow.

Mark followed the sound of the saw and found us in the woods.

"You don't have to help," I told him as Chuck and I began grabbing up the stove-length chunks of wood falling away from Daddy's saw and piling them in the trailer.

"But I want to. The faster you get done, the faster you can come over to the house. I thought we'd build snow forts today. The snow's just right."

We had the tree loaded in the trailer in no time, and then back at the house, we stacked the wood neatly along the edge of the back porch.

Mark ate lunch with us at our crowded table in the kitchen. As usual everybody fought for talking time. Charlotte, who had been allowed to join the newspaper staff, was full of ideas about the stories she was going to write. Cynthie wanted to tell about the ball game she'd been to the night before. More than once it seemed as if everybody was talking and nobody listening. Only Mark hardly said a word unless somebody asked him a question. Then to top off the meal, Chuck spilled his milk in Cynthie's lap.

As we walked across the fields to Mark's yard where he said the snow was better for making forts than in our yard, I said, "I'm sorry everything was so crazy at lunch."

"Crazy? Noisy maybe, but I liked it," Mark said. "Something's always going on around your house."

"You can say that again."

"Something's always going on around your house," Mark said with a grin.

"Please, don't say that again. You should have been there before Cathy got married. Then there were three of them to gang up on me."

"Don't they ever tease each other or Chuck?"

"Not Chuck." I looked up at Chuck who was running ahead of us and grabbing up snow to throw at us every once in a while. He nearly always missed. "Chuck is Mama and Daddy's bonus kid. He was sort of a surprise since they'd decided four kids were enough. Actually one more than enough."

"What do you mean? One more than enough."

"Do you think they would have had me if they'd known I was going to be a girl? They already had three girls."

"And if Chuck had been a girl, I guess they would have sent him back."

"Don't be silly. You can't send babies back. But if you could, they would have probably traded me in on a boy."

"You're the one being silly," Mark said.

"No, just honest with myself. Before Chuck was born, that's all everybody talked about. That this one just had to be a boy. All that talk seemed to echo in my brain as if I'd heard it all before."

"Now you're being odd."

"Silly, odd, different. That's me. The odd man out."

"Poor, pitiful Ginny," Mark said. "What else can I call you?"

"Crazy? Weird? Strange?"

"None of those. How about invisible? I looked all over the woods for you this morning after I called and Charlotte told me you must have gone for a walk. I couldn't find you."

"I was there," I said, turning away from him to stare off at the trees. "We must have just missed each other."

"I don't see how. Our woods aren't that big, and I couldn't even find tracks."

"Then maybe I was hiding from you," I said.

"Were you?" He gave me a funny look.

I had to bite my tongue to keep from telling him I'd been to see Miss Eleanore. While I hadn't minded keeping the secret from my family, somehow I didn't like not being able to tell Mark, but I had promised. I grabbed up a handful of snow, threw it at him, and then ran.

Over my shoulder I called back to him, "Of course I wasn't hiding. You just couldn't find me."

My snowball hit him right below the chin. Grabbing up some snow, he chased after me. Chuck joined in the attack, and it wasn't long before I had to plead for mercy.

We didn't build snow forts, after all. Instead, we made snow people—a mother, father, daughter, and son. The ideal family.

"I hope they don't melt," Chuck said.

"Snowmen always melt," I said. "Sooner or later."

"Well, I don't want these to melt for a long time."

"Maybe they won't, kid," Mark said. "It's still pretty cold and supposed to get colder tomorrow. Maybe they'll freeze into solid chunks of ice and stay here till spring."

I looked at the sun that was beginning to sink in the west. "I guess we'd better start home, Chuck."

"Not yet," Mark said. "It won't be dark for a couple of hours. Come on in, and we'll fix hot chocolate or something."

"Are you sure your mother won't mind? We're awful wet."

"Mom's not here, but she won't care if we stay in the kitchen and leave our boots on the porch."

I'd never been in Mark's house. He always came to my house, and though we sometimes played basketball here, if we wanted a drink Mark always brought it outside to us. The house, while not exactly a mansion, was an impressive, new-looking brick, larger than our rambling farmhouse. Now both Chuck and I fell silent as we followed Mark inside.

The kitchen gleamed with appliances. Everything was spotless except where we were dripping snow off our jeans onto the floor. A deep gold carpet crept away from the open doorway to the rooms beyond, and through that door I glimpsed white couches with deep cushions and a television with doors that closed in front of the screen.

"Maybe we'd better just go on home," I said. "We're dripping all over your mother's clean floor."

"That won't matter. Stella comes in to clean tomorrow, anyway."

"Stella?"

"Yeah. She comes in once a week to clean since Mom is so busy at the office helping Dad." Mark turned on the hot-water faucet and let it run while he got the cups and a box of hot-chocolate mix out of the cabinet.

"Where's your stove?" Chuck asked. He tracked all the way across the kitchen to peek into the living room.

"Stay in the kitchen, Chuck," I said sharply. Chuck came back to stand with me in the middle of the floor.

"He's not going to hurt anything, Ginny," Mark said. "And here's the stove, Chuck." Mark pointed at the electric range.

"The other stove," Chuck said. "The one that keeps the house warm."

"We don't have a stove like that. Our heat comes down from the ceiling like sunshine. All we have to do is turn that little knob on the wall over there."

Chuck's eyes widened as he looked up at the ceiling. "Wow," he said.

I gave his shoulder a little shake. "Don't be silly, Chuck. You've heard of electric heat before."

We sat on shiny red stools at the gleaming bar and drank the instant chocolate without saying very much. Chuck and I got even quieter when Dr. and Mrs. Shelley came in before we left.

Mark's mother glanced at the drying puddles between us and the door, then at Chuck and me, and finally let her eyes settle on Mark. "You know you're not supposed to have company in the house when we're not home."

My face flushed, and I slid off the stool as though it had suddenly gotten hot.

"We were just having a cup of chocolate and warming up a little," Mark said.

"That's all right, Mark. We've got to go anyway," I said. "Come on, Chuck."

"But I'm not through with my chocolate," Chuck said.

"We've got to go, Chuck. Now."

"Let the boy finish his chocolate," Dr. Shelley said from the doorway. He looked tired, but his voice was friendly.

Chuck settled back on the stool and lowered his head over his chocolate again. I knew it would take dynamite to move him until every drop was gone. I shifted back and forth on my sock feet and was glad that I'd at least changed into a pair of socks without a hole in them.

"We'll talk more about this later, Mark," his mother said. Then she turned to me. "You children do come back sometime when we're home." She sort of lifted the corners of her mouth in a polite smile before she disappeared down the gold-carpeted hallway.

As I stared down at my toes inside my socks and listened to Chuck slowly sip his chocolate, I planned how I was going to kill him the minute we got out of sight of this house.

After an awkward silence, Dr. Shelley said, "Those are pretty nice snowmen out there."

"It's a mother and father and son and daughter," Chuck said. "I made the boy all by myself."

When Chuck finally finished his chocolate, Dr. Shelley offered to drive us home.

"No, thanks anyway," I said. "We like going through the fields."

Mark walked back almost to the tree house with us, but we were tired and wet and the sun was sinking fast. It wasn't the same as it had been on the way over.

"I'll see you tomorrow," Mark said when he turned to go back home.

I wouldn't let Chuck climb up into the tree house after Mark left but made him climb the fence into the barn lot.

"Are you mad at me, Ginny?" he asked.

"You should have left when I told you to. We could have made some more chocolate when we got home, and we were just getting Mark into trouble with his folks."

"Dr. Shelley said I could stay."

"That doesn't mean you should have stayed when I said to leave."

"I'm sorry, Ginny." Big tears came to his eyes.

I sighed, forgetting my plans to kill him. "That's all right, Chuck. Just don't let it happen again."

We were almost to the barn before he asked, "Are we poor?"

"No, of course we're not poor," I said crossly. "Whatever gave you that idea?"

"Mark's house."

"You'd seen Mark's house before."

"Not inside. It's different when you go inside. And Dr. Shelley owns the house we live in, too, doesn't he?"

"Doctors make more money than farmers, but that doesn't mean we're poor. We have enough money."

"Then I guess Mark's rich."

At supper that night I listened while Chuck told about the heat that came from the ceiling, Mark's television with doors and the kitchen with its coffee maker stuck up under the cabinet. As he talked our kitchen seemed to shrink around me.

Charlotte waited till he was through, and then she said, "Ginny certainly knows how to pick them. Not only good-looking but rich as well."

"A doctor's son. Whooie. Impressive," Cynthie said.

I pushed back from the table so hard that my chair crashed to the floor. "Shut up," I said. "Just shut up." Then I jumped over my chair and ran for the stairs.

Behind me I could hear the sisters giggling.

"Virginia Mae," Mama called, but I kept pounding up the stairs.

"Let her alone, Rose," Daddy said. "I'll talk to her later. As for you other two . . ."

I shut the door at the bottom of my stairs on the rest of his words.

Wrapped in my blanket, I picked up my book and tried to read, but my eyes strayed from the words on the page to the window. I stared out at the night and over the trees to where I could barely see the lights from Mark's house. I tried to see Miss Eleanore's lights, but no matter how I searched the trees in that direction I couldn't make out the twinkle of a light.

After a long time I heard my father's step on my stairs. I stared down at the book and pretended to be reading when he came into the room.

He hadn't been up to my room since he and Jerry had carried the furniture up the narrow stairs. I hadn't expected him to be in my room again until he came to carry the furniture down.

His head brushed the ceiling in the middle of the room, and when he passed under the overhead light, he had to duck.

"Not very big up here," he said as he sat down on the bed.

I waited, not knowing what to expect. I'd never had a talking to from my father before. Although a frown from Daddy was enough to make all of us fall silent, Mama was the one who dealt out the actual punishments.

He wasn't frowning now, but he looked tired as though the stairs had worn him out. "Well, Ginny Mae, what have you got to say for yourself?"

"I'm sorry I ran away from the table, but they made me so mad."

"Getting teased goes along with having sisters and brothers. Seems like you just have to keep sticking needles in one another and seeing how quick you can make the other one holler."

"I guess I hollered too quick."

"You need to learn to control your temper. That's part of growing up." He stood up.

"Is that all?"

"Well, I could send you to your room, but it looks like you're already here." Daddy's smile was slow but warm. He stopped before he went back down the stairs. "There is one thing. Mark's a nice boy. I don't want you taking it out on him just because your sisters have been giving you a hard time. There's nothing wrong with being a doctor's son or a tenant farmer's daughter.''

"Chuck asked me if we were poor, Daddy."

A muscle in Daddy's jaw jerked. He took a deep breath and said, "We're honest, hard-working folks, and we've never yet gone hungry or wanted for anything we really needed."

"That's what I told him."

Daddy came over and put his hand on my head. "There's all different kinds of ways of being rich, Ginny Mae, and I wouldn't trade the riches I've got for all the money in the world."

"But don't you sometimes wish you didn't have so many kids?"

"Sure, when you get into fights at the supper table and I can't enjoy your mama's good cooking, but then harvest time rolls around and you all come in right handy." Daddy laughed low, deep in his chest, and ruffled my hair.

I listened to Daddy's steps all the way back down the stairs. Then I looked back out over the trees at the faint glimmer of lights in the distance. I thought of Mark in his room with the heat coming down from the ceiling, but I was warm in my blanket with the feel of Dad's hand lingering on my head.

Chapter Five

The next morning I knew the temperature was near zero as soon as I stepped outside because of the way the air froze the inside of my nose when I took a breath. There was no school, the sixth day we'd missed due to the weather.

After helping my father measure out the feed in the stalls and get the cows into the barn, I walked through the trees to Miss Eleanore's place. The brisk wind was icy, and I had to pull my muffler up over my face until only my eyes showed.

Miss Eleanore was sweeping off the porch when I got there. Even with her bulky coats and scarves on, she looked as if the wind might pick her up and carry her away.

"This confounded snow," she said. "It keeps blowing back up around my door."

I reached for the broom. "I'll finish it for you."

"Don't mollycoddle me." She jerked the broom handle away. "If you feel the need to be helpful, you can fill my water buckets."

"Why? Are your pipes frozen up?"

"Pipes." Miss Eleanore's laugh was muffled by her scarves. "I don't have pipes, child. I have a well. Right over there."

The well bucket was weighted on one side, and when I lowered it on its rope down to the dark water, it tipped over and sank easily. I filled the two buckets and carried them back to the house, splashing a little on my gloves where the water hardened into ice immediately.

After we filled the woodbox, we went inside.

Miss Eleanore sank down in her rocker with all her coats still on, lay her head back, and shut her eyes. "This cold weather is making me feel my years, Virginia Mae."

"How many years?" I couldn't keep from asking.

A ghost of a smile slipped across her face. "You never ask a lady how old she is unless maybe she's a hundred and you want to give her the opportunity to brag on her years." She looked at me. "I'm not a hundred although I've always figured I would be someday."

"I'm thirteen."

"Ah, the beginning age." She began unwrapping the scarves from around her head and neck. "I can remember when I was thirteen. My mother let me have a taffy pull to celebrate. Have you ever pulled taffy, Virginia? No, I suppose not. How things change over a lifetime.''

I took off my boots and set them on the paper next to the door. The papers were all new, freshly spread about the room in exactly the same spots as the day before. The yellow cat streaked across the room to rub against my socks. The hawk was still in his corner, watching me, and the black cat raised up on his stool, stretched and turned his back to me before settling again on the crackling paper.

Miss Eleanore pulled her arms out of her coats and then leaned back against them to rest. ''What do you do for fun with your young beaus when they come calling, if you don't pull taffy?''

''I don't have any beaus come calling, but my sisters do. They usually go to a movie or stay home and watch television.''

''No beaus? But what about young Dr. Joseph's son? You were with him at the sledding hill.''

''Who? Mark? We're just friends.''

''The best way to start out with a beau. I had a real beau once, but he went away to the city.''

''Couldn't you have gone with him?''

''I didn't want to leave this place.'' Miss Eleanore glanced around the room, her eyes lingering here and there. ''And now I never have.''

Everything in the room was old, but not old the way our furniture was old. These were antiques. ''Were you very rich when you were a girl?'' I asked, thinking of Mark's house and realizing this house was even larger than his though it didn't seem like it here in this room, which had been closed off from the rest of the house to save heat.

"Rich?" Miss Eleanore leaned her head back and rocked for a few minutes before she answered me. "My grandfather was wealthy. He's the one who built this house. But then my father lost most of his money when the stock market crashed."

She opened her eyes and stared at me. "You know, Virginia Mae, it's a worse social blunder to ask about a person's finances than it is to ask a woman's age."

"I'm sorry. What is it polite to talk about, then?"

"The weather," Miss Eleanore said. "Every day you can get up and say, my, isn't it a lovely day, or did you ever see so much snow, or we sure could use some rain, or is it ever going to stop raining. And you can say the same thing over and over to everybody you talk to, but let me tell you, Virginia Mae, after eighty some years of talking about the weather, you get to where you don't really care whether you talk at all."

"I'd rather talk about the taffy pull you had when you were thirteen."

"Would you, now?" Miss Eleanore smiled. "See there, Midnight, I told you she was a polite youngster, and there isn't any need in you getting all huffy at her just because Sunlight likes her."

Midnight looked at her and then began licking his feet and rubbing them over his head while he watched the hawk.

"Midnight's a naughty one," Miss Eleanore said with a little chuckle. She pushed herself up out of the chair and carried her coats and scarves to a closet. "If you'll stir up the fire a little there, Virginia Mae, we'll have a cup of tea while we talk."

"Will you tell me who Richard is?" I asked as I poked the fire in the stove the way I'd seen my mother do at home.

"No. That will have to wait for a day when it's warmer. Today you'll have to be content with the taffy pull or the weather."

I shoved a new chunk of wood in on top of the glowing coals. A spatter of sparks exploded from the coals and out on me. All Mama's warning about catching my clothes on fire screamed inside my head, and I jerked back from the sparks even as they landed harmlessly on my arm and went out at once. The sparks didn't burn me, but the stove door I jammed my hand into did.

I slammed the stove door shut and then stared down at the scorched skin on the back of my hand. It was going to blister and hurt, but worse than that, what was I going to tell Mama when I got back home from a walk in the woods with a burn on my hand.

"Did you burn yourself?" Miss Eleanore pulled my hand up to look at it. "My heavenly days, child. You should be more careful."

"Do you have some ice? Mama says that sometimes keeps a burn from getting any worse."

Miss Eleanore laughed softly. "No pipes. No wires."

I stared around the dim little room and realized for the first time that the kerosene lamp on her table was not just for decoration. "You mean you don't have electricity?"

"Folks managed for years without it. I'm still managing. They wanted to run wires back here some time back, but I told them just to run their wires off somewhere else. The kind of things wires bring with it makes a body soft."

"I don't see how you can do without electricity," I said. Then my hand began hurting, and I pulled it away from Miss Eleanore to blow on it. "I'll get some snow to put on it. That should be as good as ice."

Miss Eleanore grabbed my hand again and wouldn't let go. "That might cool it, but I've got something better if you think you can stand it hurting even worse for a few seconds."

"What? Some kind of salve?"

"No. I can take the fire out of it for you."

"How?" A funny little shiver shot through me as I met her eyes.

"The how's not for you to worry about. Just stand still and be ready for a right sharp hurting. But then it'll be gone, and you won't feel it anymore."

Mumbling something, she put her fingers to her lips, then touched the burn on my hand lightly. I tried to make out what she was saying, but if there were words in the sounds coming from deep inside her, I didn't recognize them. Then the burn on my hand felt like it was bursting into open flames, and I could think of nothing but the pain. As quickly as it came, the pain was gone.

"There," Miss Eleanore said and dropped my hand. "It won't bother you anymore."

I rubbed my fingers over the burn. It felt hard, but it no longer hurt and no blisters were rising.

Miss Eleanore picked the kettle up off the stove and poured hot water into two cups she set out on the little table. After dipping the tea bag in one cup a few times, she put it in the other cup and carried it over to her rocker. "There's sugar on the table, Virginia Mae, if you want it."

I was still standing in the middle of the floor, staring at my hand and waiting for it to start hurting again. The place that had looked scorched a moment ago was barely red now. "Was that magic?" I whispered.

"Magic?" Miss Eleanore took a sip of her tea without removing the tea bag. "No, my dear. Hardly magic."

"But it doesn't hurt anymore."

"My grandfather had many powers. Mine next to his are slight, but still useful at times. Especially this one of taking the fire out of burns."

"Have you done it before?"

"My dear, I'm an old lady. You don't learn new tricks at my age." She pointed at the table. "Your tea will be cold."

I picked up the cup and sat down without taking my eyes off of her. My hands were trembling so much that the cup clattered on the saucer.

The old lady sighed. "Do be careful, Virginia Mae. I don't want to have to take the fire out of another burn for you today."

I kept staring at her as she rocked back and forth. The sound of her rocker was steady and somehow reassuring.

"How did you do it?"

"Oh, Virginia Mae, you waver so. First fearful and then curious. I believe I do like the curious side of you best though."

"And what did you say?" I asked.

Miss Eleanore smiled. "I can't tell you. If I did, I'd lose the power, and I'm not ready to give it up yet."

"But you have done it before?"

"Many times. In years past, before people began to put the old-time cures behind them, the people around called on me often. Even those that thought it had to be the work of the devil would come when the burn was bad enough."

"Is it the work of the devil?"

"My grandfather called it a gifting from God. A gift of good and I should never misuse it."

"How could you misuse it?"

"You are full of questions. Maybe I'll go back to liking you better fearful. Now drink your tea, and don't pester an old woman to death with questions best left unanswered."

I bit back my questions, and after a few minutes she began telling me about the taffy pull she'd had when she'd been thirteen. As I listened to her words, I felt as though I'd left my old familiar world and entered a different world where things didn't have to make sense, where hawks sat quietly on perches in the corner, newspapers made carpets and burns disappeared just because you told them to.

When I let myself in the back door, Mama frowned at me from the stove. "Where have you been, Ginny? Don't you know a person staying out in this wind could freeze their lungs? I was just getting ready to send your father out to search for you."

"I wouldn't freeze, Mama. I was walking."

"Then you ought to be right tired out," she said and gave me a funny look. "You've been gone at least two hours."

"I didn't know what time it was, and the snow's really pretty with the wind blowing it around. It kept shifting around my feet, like sand in a desert windstorm."

"You're a strange one, Ginny Mae. Dreaming up the desert out in a cold wind like that." Her eyes were still stern on me. "I'd say you'd been over at Mark's."

"I wouldn't do that, Mama. Not unless his mother said it was okay first," I said quickly.

"You didn't let me finish. I would have thought that except that Mark's here."

"Here?"

"He's watching television with Chuck. He said he looked for you in the woods, but he couldn't find you." Again, Mama's eyes on me were suspicious, but she let it pass with no more questions.

"Have you ever made taffy, Mama?" I asked as I hung up my coat.

"Years ago when I was a girl," Mama said with a faint smile of memory on her face.

"Could Mark and I make taffy today?"

"It makes a terrible mess, Ginny." Then she sighed. "But then, what's a little more mess on a day like this when everybody's cooped up inside. A taffy pull might be just the thing."

"You weren't in the woods," Mark said when I sat down beside him on the couch. Chuck sat on the floor, his eyes glued to the television set.

"I know," I said.

"Then where were you?"

"I walked another way." I rushed on. "Mama says we can make taffy if you want to."

"I thought we were friends, Ginny."

"We are. The kind of friends who make taffy together."

Mark's eyes showed he was hurt. "I thought we were the kind of friends who didn't lie to each other."

I glanced around the room, glad that Chuck was totally absorbed in his program and that Cynthie and Charlotte were nowhere in sight.

"I'm sorry, Mark. I just can't tell you. I promised."

"Who could you promise?"

"Please, Mark. I'd tell you if I could."

He looked at me for a long time while my heart chunked crazily around inside of me. I didn't want

Mark to be mad at me, but I couldn't tell. I'd promised Miss Eleanore.

Finally he said, "I don't know how to make taffy."

Pulling the taffy was just as messy as Mama had predicted it would be, but it was also just as much fun as Miss Eleanore had said it was when she'd been thirteen. Mark and I pulled and joined our candy back together, touching sticky hands each time, and finally the color of the candy began to whiten and the ridges formed by the pulling didn't melt away.

We cut it up into pieces and wrapped it in wax paper. Chuck helped with the wrapping though he ate one for every two pieces he wrapped. I sneaked a few pieces down in my pocket to save for Miss Eleanore.

By the time I walked halfway home with Mark that afternoon, things were almost the same between us as they had been before—before I'd realized the difference in our families, and before he'd realized I was keeping a secret from him about my early morning walks. Almost the same, but not quite.

"Making the taffy was fun, wasn't it?" I asked.

"Yeah, maybe we can do it again sometime at my house."

"Maybe," I said, but I couldn't imagine doing anything as messy as making candy in his mother's spotless kitchen.

Today I was the one who hesitated as we parted and then said, "See you tomorrow?"

"When will you be back from your walk?"

I started to tell him I wouldn't go for a walk the next day, but then I thought of Miss Eleanore leaning back in her rocker, too tired to take off her coats until she rested, and I thought of her empty woodbox and the taffy in my pocket. Last of all the little patch of hardened skin on my hand tickled. There would have been sore blisters there if Miss Eleanore hadn't taken the fire out of it. So I said, "About the same time as today."

"Okay. Come on over to my house and we'll clean off the drive and play basketball. I'll probably have to go to practice tomorrow afternoon if it doesn't snow anymore, and I haven't touched a basketball for two days."

Since Chuck had stayed at the house to watch television, we were alone. I reached over and touched Mark's gloved hand. "Thanks."

"For what? Asking you over to play ball?" He looked a little uneasy.

"I don't know for what. For being my friend, I guess." I could feel my cheeks warming even though the wind was still bitter cold.

After what seemed like a long time he turned his hand over under mine until we were holding hands. "I like you, Ginny, more than I've ever liked any girl I've known. Let's always be friends."

Nodding, I gave his hand as much of a squeeze as our bulky gloves would allow. Then we both yanked our hands back close to our sides. After a quick goodbye, we practically ran back toward our houses.

The cold wind on my face was welcome, and I hoped it would blow away the flush on my cheeks be-

fore I got back to the house and had to face Cynthie
and Charlotte.

I wondered if I'd be able to keep from blushing
scarlet the next time the sisters started teasing me
about Mark. The thought of their laughter was
enough to make me wish I could stay out in the snow
forever.

But I finally knew what the sisters were feeling when
they got that dreamy smile on their faces while they
were talking about a certain boy. I had a boyfriend.
That's what this funny little warmth inside me had to
mean, but it wasn't altogether a pleasant feeling. I was
afraid that weird feeling might just change things between me and Mark more than even my secret visits to
Miss Eleanore or his big house and riches.

Still as I took off my boots and sat them out on the
back porch, I knew I didn't want the feeling to go
away.

Chapter Six

With her eyes closed, Miss Eleanore leaned back in her rocker while she let the taffy melt in her mouth. When at last the piece of candy was gone, she opened her eyes and said, "I thank you, Virginia Mae. That was delectable."

"Was it as good as what you made?"

"Ah now, child, nothing could ever be as good as I remember that taffy being on my thirteenth birthday. So many other good feelings are wrapped up in the memory of the taste of that taffy, but this comes very close. It's like a gift."

Fastening her eyes on me, she sat forward in her rocking chair while her smile faded. "That's what you are, Virginia Mae. A gift." Her eyes were sharp, penetrating like the hawk's. "You've been sent to me for a purpose."

I was glad Sunlight was in my lap so that I could concentrate on running my hands down his soft yellow fur and not have to meet her eyes. But she was still staring at me minutes later when I looked up.

Then seeing my eyes, she shook her head a little. She was pale, and her chin trembled.

"Are you sick, Miss Eleanore?" I asked quickly.

Sunlight leaped down from my lap to go lean against her legs. Midnight had already jumped into her lap. It was the first time I'd seen the black cat off his paper-covered stool.

"Now, it's all right, dearies," she said softly as she stroked Midnight. "If the time has come, then it's come. Sooner than we thought perhaps, but Providence is taking care of us." She looked up at me. "Would you stoke the fire and make me a cup of tea, Virginia Mae? And perhaps we could share another piece of that fine taffy."

After that I pirated away a few extra cookies or brownies and once even a piece of lemon pie to carry to Miss Eleanore's. Mama knew I was stealing food, but she didn't say anything about it. I figured she thought I was giving it to Mark.

Visiting Miss Eleanore was easier once the snow melted away enough that we could go back to school again. Then I went for my walk right after school while Chuck watched his afternoon cartoons and Mark practiced basketball.

But on Saturday, I went early in the morning again. It was a beautiful day, the sun out warm and bright with the air feeling more like springtime in spite of the patches of snow still clinging to the shadows of the barns and trees. Waiting around for more, Dad said.

Miss Eleanore met me out by the big oak tree that I'd hidden behind and watched her house that first day.

"Good morning, Virginia Mae," she said brightly. In spite of the warm sun she still wore her layers of coats and scarves. "A day like this is a gift to warm our spirits and strengthen us for the rest of the winter."

"It probably won't last long," I said. "The weatherman is promising cold weather again tomorrow."

"Don't ruin a gifting by measuring it. Just enjoy."

"Okay." I took off my sock hat and turned my face up toward the sun. "It is pretty."

"And a perfect day to introduce you to Richard and his friends."

I looked eagerly at Miss Eleanore, half expecting her to call deer, raccoon, or other wild animals out of the trees around us.

"This is Richard," she said as she stepped close to the trunk of the oak tree and patted its bark.

No squirrel scampered down the trunk. No bird flew down to perch on her arm. She kept talking. "He's been my friend ever since I can remember. Always here, strong and mighty even when I was but a child, though age is beginning to show on him as well as on me. He's lost a few limbs in the storms of late."

"The tree? Richard is the tree?"

Her eyes flashed at me. "And why shouldn't a tree have a name the same as a cat or dog?"

"I don't know. I just never heard anybody name a tree before."

"I named Richard when I was younger than you are, and he's stood guard over this place through all these years. Now it seems likely he'll still be standing guard when I am no longer here."

"I thought you said you'd never leave this place."

"Sometimes we're given no choice, but don't frown so, Virginia Mae. It'll give you wrinkles where you don't want wrinkles," Miss Eleanore said. "There's time yet. More than enough time to meet the rest of my friends."

She gave the big oak a last pat and moved away among the other trees. The maples were Thomas and Susannah. Then as we walked around the house, she reeled off names faster than I could remember them. Sally, Joseph, William, Jemma, Granville, Ivaleen, and more. She touched each tree and spoke its name as though greeting an old friend.

She'd named only a few of the cedars for she said they sprang up and grew too rapidly to name. She called them hobbledehoys.

Last she stopped by a young sapling. "This little fellow has been fighting up toward the sunshine for several seasons now."

"What's its name?"

"I never name them until I'm sure they are going to be able to establish their place here among the others, but now I think I can be confident that this tree will be strong. I named it yesterday. Virginia, meet Virginia.''

It took me a minute to understand what she meant. "Oh, you named it for me."

Miss Eleanore laughed. "And so you see why I have the reputation of turning trespassers into trees. I just did the same for you."

"I don't mind."

"Good."

"Do you have an Eleanore?"

"No, but I had a Nell one time. She got diseased, and I had her cut down for firewood. She was a nice old tree."

I tried to remember her chant of names. "How about an Ann or Annie?"

The sun disappeared under a cloud, and shadows fell across the woods. Miss Eleanore's face too was shadowed as she looked at me. "Yes. There was an Annie, but she got struck by lightning."

"Do you think that will happen to this Virginia?" I asked and looked at the little tree.

"No, I don't think so. This little tree has too many big, strong trees around it to draw the lightning away from it. It's biggest threat is that rabbits might chew away too much of its bark."

I was sorry I'd mentioned the name Annie. It seemed to take the joy out of the day for Miss Eleanore, and I was ashamed of the curiosity that had driven me to ask. But the mystery of what happened to little Annie still bothered me even though I knew

Miss Eleanore well enough now to know that she could never have harmed a little girl.

The sun edged back out from under the cloud, chasing away the shadows under the trees, but Miss Eleanore looked tired now as she moved through the woods.

"I brought some oatmeal cookies," I said. "Why don't I get in the wood, and then we can have a cup of tea."

Miss Eleanore nibbled on her cookie, sipped her tea and stared at the sunshine streaming in through the window. "Did you like my friends, Virginia Mae?"

"I've always liked trees, but I never thought of them exactly as friends before."

"Why not? They shade you in the summer, warm you in the winter, their new buds give you hope in the spring, and their fall colors lessen your sorrow over the loss of summer when autumn comes. There have been times when the trees were the only friends I had."

I watched the dust motes dance in the sunshine and didn't know what to say.

"Especially after little Annie died," Miss Eleanore added.

The sun fell full on Miss Eleanore in her rocking chair, and I could see the tracings of blue veins under her white skin. Here was my opportunity to find out all about little Annie, and I couldn't ask even one question.

"What have you heard about little Annie?" Miss Eleanore finally asked me.

"Hardly anything. I'm sorry I asked about her out there in the trees."

"But, my dear, that's a large part of your charm. Your inquisitiveness. But now you're not telling me the truth about what you've heard."

"They say that you killed little Annie," I said reluctantly before I rushed on. "But that can't be true. I know that can't be true."

The saddest look I'd ever seen settled on Miss Eleanore's face. "But I'm afraid it is, Virginia Mae."

I waited for her to say more, to explain, but she stared straight ahead without saying another word. Her cup tipped over and the tea spilled on the floor, but she didn't seem to notice. The black cat sat up on his stool and glared at me before he hopped lightly over into Miss Eleanore's lap.

The clock began to strike the hour. The sound echoed in the silent room.

When the last chime had faded away, I said, "I guess I'd better be getting on home. Mama probably has chores for me. She's sure to want to clean house or something what with all this sunshine."

Miss Eleanore began stroking the cat. She still didn't look up at me, and I wasn't sure she'd heard a word I'd said.

After pulling on my muddy shoes, I paused at the door and looked back. Somehow the bright sunshine changed the room, made it look dirtier and older even though the papers spread out were crisp and new. And the hawk, preening his feathers in a shaft of sunshine, looked odder than ever.

"Goodbye," I said. "I'll see you tomorrow."

Miss Eleanore still didn't look at me, but she said, "It would be just as well if you didn't come anymore, Virginia Mae."

I closed the door behind me and walked across the yard, past Richard and all the other trees I had just met. The ghost of little Annie followed me all the way through Miss Eleanore's woods back to the fence.

She had been five when she died. That was all I'd been able to find out about her, but now I built a picture of her in my mind. Short dark hair, brown eyes, a cute little smile, maybe even a few freckles. Why had she died? Had she been sick?

I remembered Miss Eleanore's face as she admitted to killing little Annie. A chill shook through me, and I stopped to look behind me to see if maybe there really was a ghost lurking in the trees. There was nothing but the sunshine, tracing shadows through the bare tree limbs.

I stood there at the fence and stared back through the trees to where I could barely see the shape of Miss Eleanore's house. She'd told me not to come back. Tears came to my eyes, but I shook them away along with the image of little Annie's ghost.

Once over the fence, I began running through the woods toward my house.

I was almost under the tree house when legs appeared through the opening and Mark jumped down in front of me.

"What's the matter?" he asked.

"Nothing." I stopped and caught my breath.

"You were running."

"So, is there anything wrong with that? I like to run."

"But you were running like something was after you." Mark looked back at the trees behind me.

"No, I wasn't. I was just running. In fact I'll race you the rest of the way to my house."

"I'd beat you by a mile." Mark caught my arm as I started past him. He stood in front of me and looked into my eyes. "What were you doing on Miss Nellie's property?"

"I just wanted to see what her house looked like up close." I slid my eyes away from his.

"You saw what it looked like the first day you went over there last week. You think I don't know that that's where you've been going when you disappear on these crazy walks of yours."

"So? What if it is?"

"So my father says we shouldn't bother Miss Nellie."

"I haven't been bothering anybody," I said.

"What would you call it? Spying on an old lady."

"Spying?" I yanked my arm away from him. "You're the one who does the spying. Spying on me from up there in your lookout post."

"I guess I can sit up in my tree house if I want to."

I stared at him and then the tree house. "You can't see Miss Eleanore's fence from up there. You've been following me."

"Miss Eleanore? Who's she? I thought we were talking about Miss Nellie."

"We are. That's what I said. Miss Nellie."

"No, you didn't."

"Well, what if I did and what if I didn't? Do I have to explain everything I say?" My face was flaming, and an odd trembling feeling was soaking down through my legs.

"I thought we were friends," Mark said.

"Friends don't spy on one another."

"They don't lie to each other, either." He turned his back on me and started to walk away.

I wanted to stop him and say something that would end this fight we were having, but I couldn't tell him the truth. I'd promised Miss Eleanore the visits would be our secret.

"Mark," I called. He stopped but didn't turn back around. I apologized to his back. "I'm sorry, Mark. I didn't aim to make you mad."

He half turned to look at me. "Saying you're sorry is easy, but if you were really sorry, you'd tell me the truth."

"I didn't lie to you."

"Maybe not, but I'm warning you to stay off Miss Nellie's property."

"You're warning me?"

"It's my father's farm, and he won't let you bother Miss Nellie. He'll make your father stop you."

The blood drained out of my face, and I got cold all over. "Your father may own the land, but he doesn't own me or my father."

I climbed the fence and walked across the pasture by the barn without looking back once.

I stayed mad all day as I helped Mama clean house. I'd rather have been getting up wood so that I could have thrown the chunks of wood around, but I had to be content with attacking the layers of dust in the living room.

When Cynthie and Charlotte came home from the science fair at the high school late that afternoon, they were too busy talking about their day to pay any attention to me. I should have known it was too good to last.

We were putting the last of the dishes away after supper when Charlotte turned on me. "Guess who was at the science fair, Ginny?"

"I don't know. Lots of people, I imagine."

"But one special person," Cynthie said. "Markie."

"You should have come with him. It would have been almost like a date," Charlotte said. "And all the other kids there could have seen what a catch you've made."

"I didn't want to go or I would have gone with you two," I said, biting the inside of my lip.

"You mean he didn't ask you to go with him," Cynthie said with raised eyebrows. "I thought where Mark was, Ginny was."

Charlotte looked closely at my face. I turned away but not quickly enough. She said, "Aw, Ginny and Mark have had their first little fight. Isn't that cute?" She laughed.

Mama wasn't quick enough tonight. I flew into Charlotte with both fists. Too surprised to catch herself, she fell back against the wall.

"Ginny Mae," Mama said sharply. "Go to your room right now."

I walked slowly out of the kitchen and up the stairs to my room. I didn't unclench my fists until I was in front of my window. Then I spread my hands out on the window sill and looked first at Mark's house and then toward Miss Eleanore's. After a long time I laid my head over on my hands and cried.

Chapter Seven

I woke up the next morning with a terrible cold. I was glad, because by the time I had sneezed three times, even I couldn't tell if my eyes were red from the cold or from crying.

I still felt like crying when I looked out my window, but I didn't. Instead I tried to think mean thoughts about Mark and to tell myself I was better off not having to go over to Miss Eleanore's and pack in her wood. I had enough chores to do here at home.

But no matter how I tried, I couldn't stop thinking about how many trips she'd have to make to the woodpile and back to fill up her woodbox. Finally I looked at myself in the bathroom mirror and whispered fiercely, "She told you to stay away."

When I went down to the kitchen, I apologized to Charlotte without Mama telling me I had to.

"That's okay, Ginny," Charlotte said, looking at me in a new way.

"I'll wash the dishes for you when it's your turn this week," I said. "For two weeks if you want me to."

"You don't have to do that."

A fit of sneezing made my eyes and nose run. Mama came over and laid her hand on my forehead. "I think you'd better stay inside today," she said.

Charlotte brought me a glass of orange juice, and Cynthie, without being asked, went all the way up to my room to bring down my pillow and the book I was reading. I kept waiting for one of them to start in on me about Mark again, but they just kept looking at me in that different way as though I'd sprouted horns overnight.

I lay on the couch and felt sorry for myself while I hid behind my cold. This way I didn't have to decide if I would go back to Miss Eleanore's. This way I didn't have to take the chance of meeting Mark out somewhere in the woods. In his woods, I reminded myself, but I couldn't get as mad today as I'd been able to yesterday when our fight was fresher in my mind.

The flash of anger was too quick. Mostly I just felt a funny sick feeling inside me whereas last week there'd been that excited little flutter that had let me know I had a boyfriend.

I didn't have anything now but a cold.

Even though I tried to hang on to my cold, by Tuesday I was well enough to go back to school, red nose and all. I saw Mark in the hall, but he looked the other way when I started to speak. As I went on to my next class, I remembered our fight under the tree house, but no matter how I played the words over in my head, I still felt as if I had the most right to be mad. If I was ready to say hello and forget about it, he should be, too.

After school, Mama sent me and Chuck to the woods to help Dad load wood. The weather had turned sharply back to winter.

Walking across the barn pasture, Chuck complained about missing his TV programs. Then he brightened as he said, "Maybe Mark will come help us like he did the last time we got up wood."

"I don't think so," I said.

"Why not?"

I shrugged. "I guess he's mad at me."

Chuck frowned. "What did you do to him?"

"I didn't do anything to him."

"Can't you say you're sorry?"

"I didn't do anything to be sorry about," I said, my patience running out. "He should tell me he's sorry."

Chuck stared up at me and then down at the ground. "But couldn't you say you're sorry anyway just so Mark wouldn't be mad anymore?"

"I sort of tried that already." I put my arm around Chuck's shoulder and hugged him a little. "But even if Mark's mad at me that doesn't mean he's mad at you. You can still walk over there sometimes and shoot baskets with him.''

"Mama wouldn't let me go without you."

He pulled away from me and trudged on across the field.

Daddy was sawing through the last chunk of the tree trunk when we got there. He turned his saw off and sent Chuck back to the house to get his axe. When Chuck was out of earshot, Daddy turned to me and said, "This will give us a chance to talk."

I looked up at him while my heart began to speed up inside me.

Looking out over the fields, Daddy let his eyes rest on the cows who were picking at the round rolls of hay in the barn pasture.

"This is a good place," he said. "The land's flat, and there aren't any rocks to speak of. The house is big enough to give all you kids a little elbow room. And best of all, the herd is good."

"I wish it was really ours."

His eyes left the cows and settled on me. "We'll have our own place one of these days, Ginny Mae. Could be that if we can stay here for a few years, what with the good land here and all, that we'll be able to save up enough for a down payment. Maybe not on a farm like this, but on land that will be our own."

"You think so, Daddy?" Hope lit up my eyes.

"I don't know why not. Dr. Shelley's a generous owner. He won't mind buying a little fertilizer to make the crops grow."

The fact that Daddy was confiding in me made me feel warm inside. Maybe being thirteen did make a difference.

Dad picked up a piece of bark and began whittling shavings off it. After a few minutes, he cleared his throat. "About these walks you've been taking, Ginny Mae."

The warm feeling drained away as I fastened my eyes on the shavings falling from his knife. "What about them?"

"I've been hearing some stories I don't like," he said slowly.

"What?"

"That you've been worrying the old lady who lives by herself over the way." He nodded in the direction of Miss Eleanore's house.

"I haven't been worrying her."

"Dr. Shelley says you have."

"Did Mark tell him that?" I clenched my fists, mad enough to hit somebody again.

"Hold it right there, Ginny Mae, and don't let your temper get away from you."

I took a deep breath.

"Now tell me about these walks," Daddy said as he began whittling again.

"I just went over there to thank her for taking my warts away." I held out my hand so Daddy could see that the warts were gone. "That day we went sledding and Chuck ran into her, she saw my warts and told me they'd be gone in two weeks."

Dad rubbed his rough fingers over the spot where the biggest wart had been. "I've heard tell of folks that could do that."

"Daddy, she can do all sorts of things," I started, but then I remembered my promise to Miss Eleanore. I wasn't supposed to tell people about our visits. "Anyway, I went over there to thank her," I finished lamely.

"Well, that's only right, I suppose, but now that the thanking's done, you'll have to stop bothering her."

"I haven't been bothering her. I can't believe Mark told his father I've been bothering her."

"No need getting mad at Mark. That's not who told Dr. Shelley you'd been bothering her."

"Then who?"

"The old lady herself asked Dr. Shelley to see that you didn't come back over to her place. The way I understand it, Dr. Shelley goes over to check on her every so often, and the last time he was there, she told him that you'd been worrying her."

"I don't believe it," I said faintly. I was remembering the taffy and her introducing me to the trees. I wanted to tell Daddy about that, but I couldn't. "She didn't act like I was bothering her."

"Could be the old woman has lived alone so long she doesn't rightly know her own mind."

"Little Annie," I said.

"What are you talking about?"

"Little Annie. All the kids are always telling stories about Miss Elean...I mean Miss Nellie having killed this little girl named Annie, but she didn't. She couldn't have. I don't care what anybody says." And that included Miss Eleanore herself.

"I don't know anything about all that. All I know is Dr. Shelley's been good to us while we've been here, and I don't want to do anything to make things change." Daddy looked up from his whittling, out across the fields again. "I wouldn't want to lose this place."

I stared at my father. "He wouldn't make us move, would he?"

He didn't answer me. He only folded his pocket-knife and shoved it down deep in his pocket as he said, "There comes Chuck. We'd better get this wood loaded before milking time."

The rest of the week passed quickly. On Thursday, Mark started speaking to me again, but I found an excuse when he asked if I wanted to come over to shoot basketball. The sisters started teasing me again, but I didn't get mad.

I was in sort of a daze. I helped Daddy milk. I played with Chuck and did the dishes when it was my turn. I went for walks in the woods. Sometimes I hoped Mark would find me among the trees so that we could walk together, but then I would remember the look in Daddy's eyes when he'd talked about not wanting to move and I was glad I didn't see Mark in the woods.

When I came in from my walks, Daddy would look up at me, but he didn't ask where I'd been. He trusted me to do as he'd asked.

I was trying. But each time I saw Miss Eleanore's trees, the pull to climb the fence and go see her again was stronger. I didn't know why she'd told Dr. Shelley I was bothering her, but I knew she'd enjoyed our visits as much as I did. After a lot of thinking, I decided I must have spoiled our friendship by talking about little Annie.

Now little Annie seemed to follow me everywhere. She got out of bed with me in the morning and lay down beside me at night. What had happened to her? Why wouldn't Dr. Shelley talk about it? Could it be possible that Miss Eleanore had really killed a little girl?

I had to know, and at the same time I knew I could never ask Miss Eleanore about little Annie again.

Late Friday night it sleeted, and when I woke up and looked out my window early Saturday morning, every limb, every fence wire, every bush was coated with ice. As the sun rose above the horizon, the ice began to sparkle.

Mama hesitated when I asked her if I could go for a walk, but then she nodded. "It looks as if it would be beautiful, Ginny, but remember it's cold. Don't stay out too long."

"I thought maybe I'd walk to the store. Do you need anything?"

"No, I've got to go in to town later if the roads clear up."

As I walked across the yard, the ice-coated blades of grass crunched and broke off under my feet. Above me the trees glittered and sparkled, but I walked as quickly as I could, not pausing once to admire the spectacle of the ice-coated world.

At the store I bought a box of doughnuts and then hurried back along our path to home. At the edge of Miss Eleanore's fence, I glanced around to make sure no one was about. I slipped over the fence, and seconds later, I was out of sight among Miss Eleanore's friends, the trees.

I'd known as soon as I got up that I'd have to go to Miss Eleanore's house. The rocks off her porch and around her woodpile and well would be covered with ice. I told myself I'd go over and fill her woodbox and draw her water and then leave. I wouldn't bother her. I'd just make sure she was all right.

I didn't hesitate by Richard, her oak tree, even for a heartbeat but plunged on toward the house.

Slipping, I almost fell on the icy stones that made a walk up to her porch, and again I thought of Miss Eleanore trying to make her way across this slick path to her woodpile and back.

I knocked on the door and called, "Miss Eleanore. It's me, Virginia Mae."

There was no answer. I knocked again. "I don't want to bother you, but I thought maybe you'd need me to carry in your wood today." I waited a minute before I called again. "Miss Eleanore."

This time Sunlight jumped up into the window and meowed at me. At least he wanted me to come in, but there was still no answer from Miss Eleanore. Maybe she was already outside doing her chores.

I stood there on the porch while the quiet of the place fell around me. The only sounds I could hear were the icy branches clicking together as a light breeze stirred the treetops, and Sunlight's cries muffled by the window.

I knocked and called out one more time. Then the black cat jumped up beside the yellow cat, and Sunlight gave him his spot in the window. The black cat stared at me before opening his mouth and meowing once.

Feeling as if I'd been ordered to come inside, I turned the knob of the door and pushed it open slowly. "Miss Eleanore, are you here?" I called.

The room was chilly. The papers scattered about the floor were rumpled and soiled, the one under the hawk full of droppings. The teakettle on the stove wasn't singing, and Miss Eleanore wasn't in her rocker. My eyes caught on the empty woodbox. No matter where Miss Eleanore was, at least I could bring in her wood before I left.

I moved back toward the door with Sunlight frantically sweeping his body around and around my legs while the black cat, Midnight, glared at me from the middle of the room.

"It's cold. Too cold, dearies."

The voice came from the next room. The black cat bounded away from me under the curtain. "Miss Eleanore?" I said, timidly pushing back the curtain to follow him.

A pile of heavy quilts hid everything but the very top of her head. "Miss Eleanore," I said again as I gently pulled back the quilts. "Are you all right?"

Miss Eleanore opened her eyes and smiled weakly. "Virginia Mae."

"I know you didn't want me to come, but I was worried about you."

"I'm sick, Virginia Mae. You must help me."

"Do you want me to go after Dr. Shelley?"

Her hand came out from under the quilts to grab mine in the same grip she'd used when she'd noticed my warts. This time the grip was so weak I could have pulled away easily, but I didn't.

"No. Don't tell him. He'd have them cart me away from here, and then I'd be truly done for."

"Then what can I do?"

"Help me get up. If I can drink some tea, I'll feel better." She started to push back the quilts.

"No, lie still." I pulled the covers back up around her thin shoulders. She was wearing a flannel shirt over her nightgown. "I'll fix the fire first."

She lay back and shut her eyes. "Yes, that's good." The black cat settled down beside her. "Providence, dearie. Providence has taken care of us again."

Midnight brushed against my hand as he settled beside Miss Eleanore. It was the first time he'd let me touch him.

I used some of the papers off the floor to start the fire. I wadded them up the way I'd seen my mother do and laid them in the bottom of the stove before I went out to search for dry wood.

When the fire was finally burning, I filled the tea-kettle and cleared away the rest of the papers, replacing them with fresh ones from the pile under the table until the room looked just as it usually did when I came in the mornings. Then I helped Miss Eleanore get up and settle into the rocking chair. She worked a brush through her long gray hair while I opened cans of cat food for the cats and the hawk.

"I'm afraid I've been neglecting my dearies the last two days. I managed to keep the fire going most of yesterday, but then I ran out of wood inside." She rested her arms before pulling the brush through another lock of hair. She looked over at me. "I'd hoped you'd come."

"But you asked me not to come anymore."

She closed her eyes and leaned back in the chair. "So I did, but only because I wanted to be sure you were coming for some reason other than to satisfy your curiosity."

"You told Dr. Shelley I'd been bothering you."

She rocked her chair forward with a faint nod. "I couldn't let him think I was getting soft, that I needed someone to help me do my chores."

When the water was hot, she asked me to hand her a tin box off the mantel. She stirred a generous pinch of the strong-smelling powder into her tea. Then with each sip, color began to flow back into her face.

"What is it?" I asked.

"Nothing magical," she said with a smile. "Just a strengthening herb. You could put some in your tea. It wouldn't hurt you, but it does make the tea bitter."

"I'll just use sugar." I sat a saucer of doughnuts on the table by her chair.

"Ah, thank you, my dear. And there may be some peaches in the cabinet. I'll eat and feel much better." She took another drink of the tea and then leaned back letting its medicine soak through her. "Not many people believe in the herbal cures anymore, but they are still sometimes useful."

"Does Dr. Shelley?"

"Young Dr. Joseph believes in hospitals and nursing homes and modern science. He laughs at the old cures."

I doubted if Dr. Shelley would laugh if he knew I was here against his orders, and with the thought came a stab of worry. Would he really make us move if he found out I'd come to see Miss Eleanore again?

"Listen!" Miss Eleanore let her cup clatter on her saucer and sat forward in her chair.

I stopped in my tracks but heard nothing but the clock, the comforting snap of the fire, the soft whistle of the kettle, and Sunlight purring at my feet. Still Miss Eleanore sat forward, straining to hear not just with her ears but with her whole body.

"Someone's out there," she said and leaned back.

"Who?" I thought first of Dad and then Dr. Shelley.

"I cannot hear that well, my child. You'll have to go out and see."

"You'll find him close to Richard," Miss Eleanore added as I pulled on my coat and went out the door.

From the porch I saw no one and heard nothing. She couldn't have heard anyone from inside the house. I started to just go back inside, but I decided to look around first so I could honestly tell Miss Eleanore I had.

I was almost to the oak tree when Mark stepped out in front of me.

Chapter Eight

What are you doing here?" Mark asked.

"I could ask you the same thing."

Mark frowned at me. "I'm here because I couldn't believe until I saw it for myself that you'd keep coming over here, bothering old Miss Nellie even after she told Dad to make you stay away."

"I don't care what you believe."

"Maybe I should just go tell Dad."

"Go ahead. Run tell your father. If you're lucky, he'll make us move, and then maybe you'll get a better bunch of tenants to spy on. Maybe one with a prettier daughter."

As I whirled around to go back to the house, Mark grabbed my arm. "I don't want you to move, Ginny.

You know that. But I don't understand why you have to keep coming over here, bothering Miss Nellie.''

He looked so sincere that I forgot to be mad. I just wanted him to understand. "Miss Eleanore needs me to help her, Mark, but she wants it to be a secret. That's why she told your father I was bothering her.''

"Why do you keep calling her Miss Eleanore?''

"That's her real name, and she's sick, Mark. I have to come over and carry in her wood for her until she gets better. Can you wait that long to tell on me?''

"But if she's really sick, I ought to get Dad so he can take care of her.''

"No,'' I said sharply. Softening my voice, I added, "Please, Mark.''

"I don't know, Ginny. Dad could help her.''

"She thinks your father would make her go to a hospital.''

"That might be the best place for her.''

"She doesn't think so.'' I began walking back to Miss Eleanore's house and Mark followed me. I wasn't sure Miss Eleanore would be happy to see him, but I didn't know what else to do.

She opened her eyes slowly when we went back in the house. "Ah, young Dr. Joseph's boy. Come in and have one of Virginia Mae's doughnuts. They're delicious.''

"He wants to tell his father,'' I said.

The skin between Miss Eleanore's eyes wrinkled. "But I thought the two of you were friends.''

I looked quickly at Mark who was staring at the hawk. "He thinks I've been bothering you,'' I said.

. . . be tempted!

See inside for special
4 FREE BOOKS offer

CROSSWINDS™

Discover deliciously different romance with 4 Free Novels from

 CROSSWINDS T.M.

Sit back and enjoy four exciting romances—yours **FREE** from Crosswinds! But wait . . . there's *even more* to this great offer! You'll also get . . .

A COMPACT MANICURE SET—ABSOLUTELY FREE! You'll love your beautiful manicure set—an elegant and useful accessory to carry in your handbag. Its rich burgundy case is a perfect expression of your style and good taste—and it's yours free with this offer!

PLUS A FREE MYSTERY GIFT— A surprise bonus that will delight you!

You can get all this just for trying Crosswinds!

FREE HOME DELIVERY!

Once you receive your 4 FREE books and gifts, you'll be able to preview more great romance reading in the convenience of your own home. Every month we'll deliver 4 brand-new Crosswinds novels right to your door months before they appear in stores. If you decide to keep them, they'll be yours for only $2.25 each—with no additional charges for home delivery!

SPECIAL EXTRAS—FREE!

You'll also get our Crosswinds newsletter, packed with news of your favorite authors and upcoming books—FREE! And as a valued reader, we'll be sending you additional free gifts from time to time—as a token of our appreciation.

BE TEMPTED! COMPLETE, DETACH AND MAIL YOUR POSTPAID ORDER CARD TODAY AND RECEIVE 4 FREE BOOKS, A MANICURE SET AND A MYSTERY GIFT—PLUS LOTS MORE!

A FREE
Manicure Set
and Mystery Gift *await you, too!*

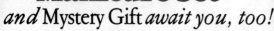

Clip and mail this postpaid card today! →

BUSINESS REPLY CARD

First Class   Permit No. 717   Buffalo, NY

Postage will be paid by addressee

CROSSWINDS
901 Fuhrmann Blvd.
P.O. Box 9013
Buffalo, N.Y. 14240-9963

NO POSTAGE
NECESSARY
IF MAILED
IN THE
UNITED STATES

"Oh dear, I have made problems for you, haven't I, Virginia Mae?" Miss Eleanore leaned back in her chair. "But you were so surely sent to me by Providence that I'm afraid I gave little thought to any problems I might cause you. And now it's causing you to lose a friend."

We both looked at Mark, but all Mark's attention was fastened on the hawk. He said, "Dad said you had a hawk, but I thought he meant a stuffed one."

"Heaven forbid." Miss Eleanore shuddered. "And I don't have Hawk. He's just resting here for a little while. Another week or two and he'll be ready to go out on his own again."

Mark pulled his eyes away from the hawk, and I could see him slowly taking in the rest of the room before his eyes stopped on Miss Eleanore. "I still think I should go get my father if you're sick."

"I'm not sick, child. I'm old, and even Dr. Joseph can't cure that."

"He'd see that you were taken care of," Mark argued.

"That's what I'm afraid of," Miss Eleanore said, and the black cat sat up on his stool and glared at Mark this time instead of me. "But Providence has already taken care of me by sending Virginia Mae. Maybe even Virginia Mae's warts were part of the plan. You know there is a plan for every life."

"Then maybe the plan was for me to follow Ginny here and then go get Dad," Mark said.

"No, not yet. I don't know why Providence brought you here. Perhaps just to muddy the waters a bit and keep things from getting dull,'' Miss Eleanore said. "Don't you think that might be it, dearies?''

Mark glanced over at me with raised eyebrows. "The cats," I explained as I poked the fire again. "I'll go get in some wood now, Miss Eleanore.''

Mark helped me fill the woodbox and draw the well water, but though he kept staring at me while we were outside and at Miss Eleanore when we went inside, he didn't say anything.

After I fixed the fire again and made Miss Eleanore another cup of tea, I looked at the clock and said, "I'd better go home before someone comes looking for me.''

"I thought somebody already had." Miss Eleanore nodded over her cup toward Mark. "Is he going to report on us, Virginia Mae?''

"I don't know." I didn't look at Mark.

"I'm not a tattletale," Mark said crossly. "But I still think you ought to let Dad come and see about you, Miss Nellie.''

"No, no." Miss Eleanore grabbed my hand. Her grip was much stronger now. "Make him understand, Virginia Mae.''

"I'm not sure I can.''

"I won't tell," Mark said.

Miss Eleanore loosed her grip on my hand and sank back in her chair with relief. "Good. Maybe I haven't caused you to lose a friend after all, Virginia Mae," she said, so softly that I could barely make out the words.

I hesitated, feeling the odd urge to lean over and kiss her dry cheek. "Are you sure you'll be all right? I might be able to stay a little longer."

"Go," she said, waving her hand at me. "And stop staring at me like that. I'm not going to die just yet. I still have the gift to get rid of, but Providence will take care of all that."

"I'll look in on you later today."

"You don't have to. I have my dearies here to take care of me." She stroked Sunlight who had hopped up in her lap.

Following Mark out on the porch, I pulled the door slowly shut behind me. I didn't care what Miss Eleanore said. I'd come back later to make sure she was still all right even if I had to tie sheets together and climb out my window.

I moved out ahead of Mark, avoiding the icy rocks, and led the way through the trees. The woods were dripping now as the sun began to warm the air.

After we'd climbed over the fence back into our field, Mark asked, "Is that what you've been doing every time you went over there?"

"This is the first time she's really been sick. The other times she was just tired. She said the snow and cold weather made her feel old."

"She is old."

"But she didn't seem like it last week when she took me around and showed me her trees." I looked back over the fence.

"Dad says she's a little crazy."

"I like her."

"Yeah, I could tell." Mark looked back at Miss Eleanore's trees too. "Did you ask her about little Annie?"

"Yes." I started walking toward my house again.

"What did she say?"

"That the stories were true. That she killed the little girl."

The ice crunched under our feet. We were almost back to the tree house before Mark asked, "When did she tell you that?"

"Last Saturday."

"And you still went back over there?"

"I don't know what happened to little Annie, but I know Miss Eleanore didn't kill her."

"But you just got through saying she admitted it."

"I don't care what she said. It's not true. It had to be some kind of mistake. Just like it was a mistake for me to stop going over there." I looked toward the barn. "I hope Daddy understands."

"I'm not sure my father will," Mark said.

"I know."

"But I won't tell him, and if he finds out, I'll tell him you were just helping Miss Nellie out."

I reached over and touched his hand. "Thanks, Mark."

"Does this mean we're friends again?"

"I thought we were always friends."

"We didn't act much like it," Mark said.

"I guess not."

"But now that we're not mad at each other anymore, why don't you come over this afternoon when it warms up a little and play some basketball?"

"Maybe. Mama and Daddy may not let me out of the house again."

"You mean because they'll think you've been over at Miss Nellie's house?"

"Your father told my father not to let me go over there any more."

"Don't worry. I'll be your alibi. Come on." He practically leaped over the fence. "I'll race you to your back gate."

"You'll scare the cows," I yelled, but it was too late. Mark was already off running across the pasture.

Dad, who was just letting the cows out of the barn, looked up at Mark tearing across the field. A couple of the cows raised their heads and dug their feet into the icy mud that surrounded the barn, but there was no stampede like I had expected. Shaking his head, Dad went back into the barn without even hollering at Mark to slow down. Still I didn't run. I'd broken enough rules for one morning.

Nobody said anything about how long I'd been gone. They were too glad to see me showing up with Mark. Especially Chuck and the sisters. But even Mama made pancakes without being asked.

After that it was easy again to slip away to Miss Eleanore's. It was the middle of the next week before Dad said anything at all about it. I had just come back from my walk and was going to the barn to help him get the cows in.

"You're not bothering that old woman again, are you, Ginny Mae?"

"I'm not bothering her, Daddy. I wouldn't do anything like that."

Daddy sighed and then put his hand on my shoulder. "I know you wouldn't, Ginny Mae."

He didn't say any more about it, and neither did I although I wanted to try to explain. I wanted to tell him how Miss Eleanore seemed to be depending on my visits more and more as the days passed. I even went to the store for her.

As the man at the store packed the cans of cat food into the sack, he said, "I didn't know you folks had a cat."

I turned away to study the candy counter without answering him. I could feel his eyes on me as he finished sacking the rest of the groceries, and I wished somebody else would come in the store to take his attention off me.

"Is that all you need, Ginny?" he asked.

I checked over the list Miss Eleanore had given me. "That's all," I said.

He took the money, and then when he handed me my change, he said, "This is for Miss Nellie, isn't it?"

I glanced around quickly, glad now that there was no one else in the store. "What makes you think that?"

"The cat food, the peaches, the tuna. Miss Nellie has been getting these same things for fifteen years, almost to the can." The man laughed. "When you run a little country store like this, you get to know your customers' tastes pretty well."

I stood there as if I'd been caught swiping one of his candy bars.

He didn't seem to notice. "Let me tell you, I'm glad to have figured it out. I was getting worried about Miss Nellie. I knew she'd have to be about out of cat food, and while she might starve herself, she'd never let her cats go hungry. Is she okay?"

"She's been a little sick, but she's feeling better." I looked up at the man. I didn't even know his name. He was just the man at the store, but I had to trust him. "She doesn't want anybody to know."

The man shook his head. "That sounds like Miss Nellie, but I suppose a person's got a right to live however they want."

"Then you won't tell Dr. Shelley?"

"Not if she doesn't want me to. In all the years I've known Miss Nellie, I've never known her to need a doctor anyway. She has better ways of healing." He handed me the sack of groceries. "Is that going to be too heavy for you?"

"I can carry it."

The man smiled. "I'm glad Miss Nellie's got somebody to see after her. Underneath that crusty old hide, she's a good-hearted woman."

I wanted to ask him about little Annie, but the bell on the door rang before I could figure out the right words for my question.

The sack of groceries got heavier and heavier as I climbed back up the hill toward Miss Eleanore's fence line. Little Annie walked along with me. I was still curious about what had happened to her, but not in the same way I'd been when Mark had first told me about the long-ago mysterious death of the little girl.

Then the story had sent chills up my spine as I'd looked around the trees expecting to see a real ghost. Now the ghost of little Annie was familiar, and if not welcome in my thoughts, at least accepted there.

As I walked through the woods, I was glad I hadn't asked the man at the grocery about her. Miss Eleanore would tell me about her someday. Until then it didn't matter if I knew the whole story.

Now I had more important things to worry about, such as Dr. Shelley finding out about my visits to Miss Eleanore or the fact that I was breaking my father's trust. But I wasn't really doing anything wrong. Miss Eleanore needed me like no one had ever needed me before.

At home if there was a chore to be done there were always hands to do it. At Miss Eleanore's I was the only one. Miss Eleanore would watch me loading up the woodbox or packing in the buckets of water, and she would turn to Midnight and say, "Providence, dearie, Providence." Then she'd look at me and smile, but the smile would be sad.

"Is something wrong?" I'd ask and notice again the blue shadows under her eyes and how pale she was. And I'd think of Dr. Shelley and wonder if he could help her as Mark kept saying he could.

"It's just that it's almost time, and I don't know if either one of us is ready no matter what Providence thinks."

"Ready for what, Miss Eleanore?"

"The gifting," she'd answer and close her eyes while her head fell back against her rocking chair. "But there's time yet. We'll talk about it tomorrow. You are coming back tomorrow?" She'd open her eyes and search me out.

"Of course I will."

"Good. Then I won't have to worry about my dearies. And we'll talk then."

Then came the Saturday afternoon when Midnight showed up in our yard.

Chapter Nine

Chuck came around the house carrying the black cat. "Look, Ginny, a cat."

I was hanging Mama's washing out on the line. When I looked over my shoulder and saw the cat, I dropped the socks and clothespins. Midnight glared at me with his smoldering eyes and fought against Chuck's hold.

"You'd better let him down, Chuck. I don't think he likes being carried."

"He likes for me to hold him." Chuck tightened his grip.

The black cat raked his claws across Chuck's hand. Chuck turned loose, and Midnight dropped lightly to his feet, looked at me, and meowed once before he streaked away across the yard.

I grabbed Chuck's arm to keep him from running after the cat. "How bad did he scratch you?"

"Not bad." Chuck tried to pull loose. "Let me go. I have to catch him before he gets away."

The three scratches across the back of his hand were oozing blood. "You'd better go wash that and let Mama put some medicine on it. She says cat scratches get infected real easy."

"But what about the cat?"

"I'll go after him, but he probably just happened to wander into our yard. I'm sure he belongs to somebody else." When tears came to Chuck's eyes, I went on. "If Mama says you can have a cat, we can surely find one nicer than that one."

"He was nice. You just scared him."

"That cat has never been afraid of anything," I said. "Now go on in and let Mama doctor your hand."

"But the cat," Chuck cried.

"I told you I'd go look for him." I waited till Chuck headed for the back door. "Tell Mama I'll be back in a little bit."

I was already to the tree house when Mama hollered at me. Pretending not to hear her, I ran on through the trees.

Midnight was waiting on the porch when I got to Miss Eleanore's house. I leaned against a post till I got my breath, but even then I was so shaky inside that when I knocked and called to Miss Eleanore, my words came in jerks.

There was no answer.

I'd been there that morning to do her chores, and she'd sat in her rocker and talked about Providence and how we'd talk tomorrow, like she did every day.

I knocked again, but there was still no answer except the impatient cry of the black cat who pushed in front of me close to the door.

With trembling hands I turned the doorknob. As soon as the crack was big enough, Midnight jumped through.

Miss Eleanore lay on the floor beside her rocking chair, her teacup in broken pieces beside her.

"Miss Eleanore?" I said softly, hesitating just inside the door. I had to make myself go kneel beside her. Her face was white and somehow crooked as if half of it had been shoved sideways when she fell.

"Please don't be dead," I whispered.

Her eyes flickered the barest bit but didn't open.

"Everything's going to be okay. I'll fix you some tea," I said.

She didn't move, but when I leaned low over her face I could feel the whisper of her breath against my cheek.

"I don't know what to do, Miss Eleanore."

Both the cats began yowling then, and even Hawk screamed at me from his corner. I looked at them and said, "I can't make her get up. She's too sick."

The cats still stared at me. "I don't know what to do," I said again, a little louder. But it wasn't true. There was only one thing to do.

I eased a pillow under Miss Eleanore's head and covered her gently with one of her quilts. "I'll be back as soon as I can, Miss Eleanore," I said as I tucked the quilt up around her neck.

I started for the door but then came back to kneel beside her again. With my lips close to her ear, I said, "I'm sorry, Miss Eleanore." Her cheek felt cool and dry when I kissed her.

It was a long run back through the woods. By the time I got to Mark's house, I could hardly breathe, much less talk.

Mrs. Shelley came to the door. "Mark's not here. Didn't he tell you that he was going to play basketball at school this afternoon?"

"I'm not here for Mark," I said between gasps for breath. "I want Dr. Shelley."

"Is someone sick over at your house?"

I shook my head. "Please, I need to see Dr. Shelley."

"What is it, Helen?" Dr. Shelley called from inside the house.

"It's one of the Todd girls."

I pushed past Mrs. Shelley to grab Dr. Shelley's arm. "You've got to come. It's Miss Eleanore."

"Are you talking about Miss Nellie?"

"Yes. Oh, please hurry."

"All right. Wait here while I get my things."

But I couldn't wait. I was back across the yard and running through the trees again. Back on Miss Eleanore's land, it seemed as if the trees held back their branches to let me pass.

When Dr. Shelley got there, I was sitting on the floor beside Miss Eleanore, holding her hand. She gave no sign of knowing I was there, but she was still breathing.

"She's had a stroke," Dr. Shelley said as soon as he saw her. "It's a good thing I called the ambulance before I left the house."

Minutes later the ambulance attendants were picking up Miss Eleanore's fragile body and placing it on their stretcher. They rolled her away, out the door, and then carried her down the steps to the ambulance.

I felt I should run and climb into the ambulance beside her, but my feet were rooted to the porch. I could only watch as one of the men closed the doors of the ambulance shutting Miss Eleanore inside.

"She'll never forgive me," I whispered.

Dr. Shelley's eyes were dark on me. "Did you do something to upset Miss Nellie, Ginny?"

I just stood there, unable to say a word.

"I told your father not to let you come over here anymore. I'll have to talk to him about this." He went down the porch steps and to his car without looking back at me.

With its siren screaming, the ambulance slipped away between the trees. I stood there like a statue long after the echo of the siren had died away.

Sunlight rubbed against my leg, but no purr rose from within him even after I leaned down and picked him up.

Back inside the house I opened a can of cat food and set it out for the cats. Sunlight barely sniffed it before he jumped up in the empty rocking chair. Midnight was nowhere to be seen, and I wondered if he had tried to follow the ambulance.

Even though the stove was still putting out enough heat to make the teakettle sing, the room felt cold and empty without Miss Eleanore. All at once I wanted to get away, to be outside in the sunshine again.

After making sure the damper on the stove was closed, I started out the door. Sunlight's sad little meow stopped me.

I looked at the yellow cat and said, "I don't know, Sunlight. I don't know when she'll be back."

Before I left I went around the house to the little maple tree that Miss Eleanore had named Virginia. The tree looked young and strong and somehow made me feel better, but then when I passed under Richard the oak on my way home, I noticed for the first time the many new limbs on the ground around him. The ice storm had been hard on him.

The clothes were all on the line when I got back home. I looked at them hanging neatly in the sun to dry and wished I could somehow get to my room without having to talk to anybody. Even as I thought it, Chuck came out in the yard to meet me.

"Where's the cat?" he asked.

"The cat?"

"You promised you'd get the cat for me."

"Oh, the cat." It seemed like days since I'd left to chase Midnight through the woods. "I told you that cat probably belonged to someone else. He did."

"How do you know? Did you find him?"

"He's Miss Nellie's cat."

"Miss Nellie." Chuck's eyes widened. "Witches' cats are always black, aren't they, Ginny? Do you think she might put a spell on me because I bothered her cat?"

"Don't be silly. She's not a witch."

"How do you know?"

"I just know. Now go away and leave me alone." Maybe I still had a chance of getting up to my room before anybody else saw me.

"Did you follow the cat all the way to her house, Ginny?" His eyes on me were bright, almost fearful as if I had changed from the sister he could count on to play with him when everybody else was too busy, to somebody strange or scary.

"What if I did? Midnight's just a cat, and Miss Eleanore's just an old lady." I felt like crying.

Mama was waiting for me at the door. One look at her face and I knew all hope of escaping to my room unquestioned was gone. Then remembering the frown Dr. Shelley had been wearing when he'd gone down Miss Eleanore's porch steps to his car, I wished I could just run off to the woods and get lost.

"Go out to the barn and help your father, Chuck," Mama said.

Mama didn't often use that tone of voice, but when she did, even Chuck knew better than to argue. He gave me a backward look over his shoulder as he went toward the barn. I followed Mama into the kitchen, glad the sisters had gone somewhere and weren't here to be part of my shame.

Mama stared at me for a long time before she said, "Have you been over there bothering Miss Nellie?"

"I never bothered her, Mama. Honest."

"But you have been over there." She waited until I nodded and admitted my guilt. "And after your father told you not to go. That's willful disobedience, Virginia Mae."

My eyes filled with tears. "I had to go, Mama. There wasn't anybody else to help Miss Eleanore, and she was sick."

"You mean Miss Nellie?" Mama frowned.

"She wanted me to call her Eleanore. She needed me, Mama, to carry in her wood and draw her water. I had to go even though Daddy said not to."

"I don't understand. Dr. Shelley said you were bothering the old lady."

"She told him that because she thought if he found out I was doing her chores that he'd think she was too old to stay by herself and that he'd find a way to make her go to a nursing home. She didn't want him to think she was getting soft."

"Ginny, none of this is making much sense."

"It made sense to her." I heard in my mind again the ambulance leaving, and the tears in my eyes spilled over. "Oh, Mama, she had a stroke. I found her when

I went over there. They took her away, and now she'll die.''

Mama gathered me in her arms. "There, there, child. Everything will likely work out all right."

I hid my face against Mama's shoulder and shook my head. "She'll never forgive me for going to get Dr. Shelley. But I had to." I looked up at Mama's face. "I did have to, didn't I, Mama?"

"You did the right thing, Ginny."

When I stopped crying she pushed me back away from her and handed me a tissue. There were tears on her cheeks too. I blew my nose and then glanced up to see her looking around the kitchen just the way Dad had looked over the fields.

"Dr. Shelley won't make us move just because of what I did, will he?"

"I don't see why he would. You were just being a good neighbor." But she didn't sound too sure of her words. "Still, he's a stern man. It could be he won't be understanding."

"What'll we do then?"

Mama's face was grim. "Stay out the year and then find a new place."

"I'm sorry, Mama. I didn't mean to make trouble."

"I know, but you should have told us right off instead of sneaking around doing what you'd been told not to do."

I hung my head. "Should I go out and tell Daddy before Dr. Shelley comes? He said he was going to come talk to Daddy."

Mama sighed and touched my cheek. "You go on up to your room, Ginny. I'll talk to your father."

From my window I saw Mama walk slowly out to the barn and then after a long time walk back to the yard and start gathering in the clothes off the line. The sisters came home, and I could hear their voices far below me as they helped Mama in the kitchen. Then I saw Daddy walk across the field to get the cows in to milk.

Chuck began packing in the wood, and the smell of supper drifted up the steps. But nobody called to me to come help. So I sat by my window, watched, listened and wished I could just dissolve into thin air.

Even Miss Eleanore didn't need me now. I'd failed her, too, by bringing in Dr. Shelley or maybe by not getting him soon enough. Perhaps if Mark had fetched his father that first day Miss Eleanore had been sick, then she might have gotten better and not had the stroke.

Daddy was coming to the house when Dr. Shelley's car pulled in the driveway. Though it was dark now, I could see them talking together in the light from the porch. I wanted to run down the stairs and ask Dr. Shelley if Miss Eleanore was all right, but I was afraid.

After Dr. Shelley drove away, Charlotte called up the stairs, "Ginny, time to eat."

It was an ordinary call, like any other night call, but I felt funny walking down the steps to join the family at the table.

Everybody's eyes were on me, and I'd never felt so set apart and different. I looked up at Daddy with the unspoken question in my eyes.

He looked tired and worn, the way he sometimes did in the summer when we were trying to get the hay in before a rain. Now he tried to smile a little as he said, "I explained it to him the best I could, Ginny Mae. He's a reasonable man."

"But Miss Eleanore," I said, the words barely a whisper. "Is she going to be all right?"

"It wasn't good news about the old lady, I'm afraid. She hasn't come around yet, and they aren't sure she will."

"I should have never gone after Dr. Shelley. She'll die in the hospital."

"She would have died for sure if you hadn't gone to get help, Ginny," Mama said.

"No. She might have come to and I could have given her some tea. The cats would have helped her. I don't know what she'll do without her dearies," I said.

Mama broke the odd hush that had fallen over the table while I talked. "It takes more than tea to help somebody who has a stroke," she said gently.

"But this was special tea. She put herbs in it." No one said anything, and after a minute I went on. "Miss Eleanore could cure all sorts of things. She made my warts go away, and once when I burned my hand, she stopped it from blistering."

They were all staring at me. Finally Chuck said, "She really is a witch."

"She's not a witch. She just has some kind of special healing gifts."

No one reached for a bowl or picked up their forks. The silence was thick and heavy, and I looked down at my plate. "I'm not hungry. Can I go back up to my room?"

I was on the first step when I heard Chuck ask, "Has Miss Nellie turned Ginny into a witch, too?"

Chapter Ten

I kept going to Miss Eleanore's every day to feed the cats and the hawk. While Sunlight always rushed to meet me at the door, Midnight only glared at me from his bed on the stool. He wouldn't go near his food while I was there, and if I tried to pet him he snarled and spat at me.

Sometimes when I was cleaning up after the hawk, I wondered if I should untether him and let him fly away. His wing seemed to be fully healed, and Miss Eleanore had talked about letting him go. But because I wanted everything to be the same when she came home, I left Hawk where he was.

I put out clean papers on the floor every day and had a fire laid in the stove ready to light. The house was ready, waiting for her just like the cats, and so was I.

The week passed slowly. No one at my house mentioned Miss Eleanore, and I was afraid to. While mealtimes had gone back to being noisy and full of talk again, I still felt set apart. The sisters didn't tease me, but treated me as though I'd been sick and wasn't quite well yet. As for Chuck, more than once I caught him staring at me, but when I asked if he wanted to play a game or something, he always shook his head and backed away. The only time he'd play with me was when it meant he'd also get to play with Mark.

But after a few days Chuck's natural curiosity got the best of him, and as we were walking through the woods to Mark's house, he asked, "Did she really cure your burn, Ginny?"

"Yes," I said.

"How?" His eyes were wide with that look I was beginning to dread whether I saw it in his eyes or in the sisters' eyes.

"I'm not sure. She touched it and said something, but I couldn't understand the words."

"Was it like a spell?"

"I don't know. I've never heard a spell."

"I'll bet it was a spell. A spell just like the ones Rachel says she uses to turn kids into trees. Did she tell you about that?"

"Miss Eleanore never turned anybody into a tree. She just names them." I tried to explain to Chuck about the trees, but the more I talked the wider his eyes grew. When I told him about the tree Miss Eleanore had named for me, he shivered and grabbed my hand.

"I don't want you to turn into a tree, Ginny."

"You mean like this." I threw up my arms in my best tree imitation, but Chuck looked so scared that I dropped them at once and laughed. "I'm not going to turn into a tree. And don't you think it's about time you grew up a little and stopped believing everything you hear?"

"Rachel says that sometimes witches pick out somebody to teach all their spells to before they die."

"What is this Rachel? A walking encyclopedia on witches?" I asked.

Chuck shrugged. "She knows lots of things."

"I'll bet she does. Tell me, Chuck." I looked straight at him. "Do you really think I'm a witch?"

He stared at me a minute before he shook his head.

"Well, I reckon not, and Miss Eleanore isn't a witch, either. I don't care what our little expert Rachel says."

"Then why does she live over there all by herself?"

"I don't know. I guess maybe she wants to." Little Annie popped up beside me in my thoughts for the first time since Miss Eleanore had been taken away to the hospital.

"Is she going to die?"

"No, of course not," I said fiercely.

"Daddy said she might. I asked him."

I'd been pushing away the same thought for days. I wanted to push it away now, but once the words had been spoken aloud, I couldn't. Miss Eleanore might die. She had power over warts and burns, but nobody could have that kind of healing power over strokes.

If Chuck hadn't been with me, I would have walked off through the trees to Miss Eleanore's house and let Sunlight rub against my legs. I would have wiped the dust off her rocking chair and swept her porch until it was clean and ready for her return. But instead I walked on toward Mark's house with Chuck trailing a little behind me, no longer talking, and the worry was like a shadow over the sun.

At Mark's house, Mark threw me the basketball as soon as he spotted us coming through the yard. Even though I was a long way from the goal, I put up a shot, anyway. The rim didn't even rattle as the ball swished through the net.

"Wow," Mark said. "How did you ever hit that shot?"

"I don't know. Chuck thinks I'm a witch, so maybe I conjured it in."

Chuck hit me on the arm. His face was red, and his eyes full of tears as he said, "I didn't say no such thing."

I looked from Chuck to Mark. "What about you, Mark? Do you think I'm a witch?"

Mark got a funny look on his face as he dribbled the ball a couple of times before he put up a shot of his own. It bounded off the rim and to the side. He looked down and then finally toward me. "You have been different since you started going over to Miss Nellie's."

I let Chuck chase after the ball. "How?" I asked, my insides fluttering nervously.

"I don't know. Like you knew something nobody else knew. Like maybe this secret of yours was more important than anything else."

"She needed me to help her, and there were reasons she didn't want me to tell anybody."

"She was using you, Ginny. I mean for years she's chased off anybody who came anywhere close to her place."

"Maybe nobody ever tried to be friendly with her before. Maybe they were all just..." I ran out of words.

"Just what?"

"I don't know. Just nosy, maybe."

"Are you saying you weren't nosy?" Mark asked. "Half the reason you went over there in the first place was so you could ask her about little Annie."

"I went over there to thank her for taking off my warts. Asking about little Annie was just something that happened one day."

Chuck, who had been dribbling the ball while he listened to us, forgot to give the ball a bounce as he stared at me. "Did you really ask her about little Annie?" he asked.

"So what if I did? Maybe I was a little nosy, but then she needed somebody to help her with her chores and it didn't hurt me to carry in a little wood for her."

"She was using you," Mark said.

"No, she wasn't. She never asked me to do anything for her. In fact, she even told me not to come back, but I couldn't stay away."

"Why not?" Mark asked.

"She put a spell on her," Chuck said, his eyes wide again.

"Hush with your spells," I said crossly. "Miss Eleanore isn't a witch, and she wasn't using me. I went over there to help her because I wanted to. Okay?"

I picked up the basketball and began pitching it back and forth in my hands. There were just some things that couldn't be explained, and the way Miss Eleanore and I had become friends was one of them.

Mark looked off in the direction of Miss Eleanore's house though he couldn't even see her trees from here. "She's a strange old lady all right. Imagine keeping a hawk in your living room."

"She probably put a spell on it, too," Chuck said.

I ignored Chuck and kept pitching the ball back and forth. "Have you heard your father say how she's doing?"

"No." Mark reached out and grabbed the ball away from me.

"Chuck said Daddy said she might die."

"She's old," Mark said. "And I did hear Dad talking about what would happen to her place if she died."

"She can't die. We haven't had our talk yet."

Mark looked at me for a minute before he said, "What talk?"

"I'm not sure. Something about Providence and gifts and her dearies."

"You're beginning to sound as strange as Miss Nellie. I think you ought to just forget all about her. There's nothing you can do for her now, anyway." He passed the basketball over to Chuck. "And I thought you two came over to shoot baskets with me."

I didn't feel like playing anymore, but I waited an hour before I told Chuck we had to go home. Chuck fussed a little, but Mark didn't try to get us to stay. He didn't walk partway home with us, either. I was beginning to wonder if that day in the woods with the snow falling around us, when we'd touched hands and promised to be special friends, had ever actually happened.

When we were almost to the trees, I looked back. Mark was standing on the blacktop drive with his basketball on his hip, staring after us. I raised my hand to wave, and so did he. As I turned back toward home, I realized he'd never really answered me when I'd asked him if he thought I was a witch.

The next day was Saturday, and when Mama said she was going to town, I asked if I could go along.

"I'm just going to the grocery," she said.

I looked down at the floor, gathered up my nerve, and said, "I want to go to the hospital to see Miss Eleanore."

Mama was quiet for so long that I looked up and begged, "Please, Mama."

She was frowning. "You realize that Miss Nellie's very sick. She may not be able to talk to you like she did before."

I saw again in my mind the way Miss Eleanore's face had been twisted when I found her. "I know, but I still have to go see her."

Mama's mouth straightened out into a funny little smile. She put her hand on my shoulder and said, "All right then, Ginny. I guess maybe you should go see the old lady, and we'll just worry about tomorrow when tomorrow comes."

"What do you mean? Did Dr. Shelley say I couldn't go see Miss Eleanore?"

"He thinks it would be best if you stayed away. He still has trouble believing you were welcome at the old lady's house."

"But I was. She needed me, Mama."

"I know," Mama said gently. "Your father and I have talked it out, and we know you weren't going over there to torment the old woman. That's not to say you weren't doing some things wrong. It's just to say we believe your motives were good."

I hung my head. "But what about Dr. Shelley?"

"Don't you worry about him. We've had trouble with landlords before. We probably will again." She raised my chin up till she could look in my eyes. "One thing you need to remember, Ginny. You children are more important to your father and me than any place could ever be."

Then before I could start crying, she dropped her hand and briskly set about getting ready to go to town.

The hospital was big, full of staring windows, and I wondered how I'd ever find Miss Eleanore's room. I was relieved when Mama parked the car and went inside with me. She asked at the desk for Miss Eleanore's room number, and then we rode up in the elevator together.

"What's that smell?" I asked as we got off the elevator on the fourth floor.

"Hospital smell. Medicine, sick people, disinfectant."

"I don't like it."

"Hardly anybody does."

"I don't think Miss Eleanore will like being here."

Mama smiled a little at me. "Nobody ever likes to be in the hospital except maybe when you're going to have a baby. Then it's different." Mama got a half-worried and half-happy look on her face. "It'll be Cathy's time soon. Last night when I talked to her on the phone, she said the doctor had told her the baby might come anytime now."

"That means I'll be an aunt," I said, thinking how strange that sounded.

"And me a granny." Mama looked at the numbers on the wall. "We need room 407."

"Will you come in with me?"

"For a minute, but if you want to visit, you can stay while I go to the store."

When we found 407, Mama stood back and let me go first. I timidly pushed open the door. Miss Eleanore, wrapped in a white blanket, was sitting in front of the window. She didn't look around when the door opened.

"Miss Eleanore," I said softly.

She slowly turned her head to look at me. When she smiled, only one side of her mouth turned up. "Virginia Mae, my own gift of Providence." Her voice was low and a little hoarse, but the words were clear.

"This is my mother," I said. "She brought me."

"That was kind of her." Miss Eleanore lifted her eyes to Mama's face.

Since there was only one other chair, I sat down on the floor beside Miss Eleanore's chair. Mama sat down in the other chair and made polite conversation about Miss Eleanore's health and the weather. After a few minutes she made her excuses and then looked at me.

"I'll stay a while if it's okay with Miss Eleanore," I said. Now that I was with Miss Eleanore, I was no longer afraid of her being sick.

After Mama left, Miss Eleanore took my hand in hers and said, "Seeing you, child, is almost as good as seeing the dearies. Are they all right?"

"They miss you. Midnight especially. And I think he and Hawk have been fighting some."

"They would without me there to make them behave. I guess the best thing for you to do, Virginia Mae, is to let Hawk free. His wing should be healed by now. I should have turned him loose already."

"But you'll be home soon. Then you can do it."

"Perhaps." Her chin sank down on her chest, and I thought she'd fallen asleep. Still her grip on my hand was tight, and I was content to sit there with her quietly.

After a long time she raised her head and said, "I wish I could have a cup of tea."

"Do you think I could go get you one?"

"Oh, they bring me what they call tea here, but it's not much more than colored water."

"When you go home, I'll come over and stay with you and make you tea whenever you want."

"Such a gift you are, child, but it will never be. This place is too clean. Nobody can live in a place so clean. I told Dr. Joseph that when I woke up, but he won't listen."

I looked down at the floor. "I had to go get him. I didn't know what else to do."

"It's all right, Virginia Mae. Unfortunate perhaps, but one can only hold back the world so long. And Joseph means well. He always has." She tried to smile at me again. "Perhaps this, too, is part of Providence's plan, for we still have not had our talk."

"Maybe you should rest now. I can come another time."

"Soon there will be nothing but rest. Still, I am tired. If you'll help me back to bed, then I'll tell you about the gifting, for surely it is time and past."

Awkwardly I helped her back into the hospital bed. In her silk gown without her flannel shirts and corduroy britches she seemed to have shrunken to nothing.

"Young Dr. Joseph brought me the gown," Miss Eleanore said as she lay her head back on the pillow with a sigh. "He means well."

I plumped her pillow and spread the cover over her. She looked sicker lying in the bed than she had in the chair, and I began to wish my mother would return.

Miss Eleanore patted the bed. "Sit here beside me. My voice is weak, and I have a lot to say."

She shut her eyes and was quiet for so long that I thought she must have forgotten that she was planning to tell me something. That once again the talk would have to wait for another day.

But then she said, "I have to do the gifting, but first you must know the cost."

"If you're too tired, I can come back tomorrow."

"No, there might not be a tomorrow for me."

"Don't say things like that. You're getting better. I'm sure of it."

"Of course I am, Virginia Mae," she said with her strange sideways smile that was both gentle and sad. "But still I want us to have our talk today. Do you remember the day you asked about little Annie?"

"I remember. I should have kept quiet."

"No, no. It was right you asked. You have to know the truth, and though it is the truth that I caused the child to die, that isn't the whole truth. Truth is so often like that. Bits and pieces that can be put together in so many different ways."

I watched her face without saying anything.

She took a deep breath. "Annie's father brought her to me. She'd been badly burned, and in those days many came to me for my gift. Young Dr. Joseph had just set up his practice in town, but not many trusted him yet. You see, he was so young, and for many years they had come to me for help with every kind of ailment." She looked at me. "I'm not a doctor, but I helped them. And if I couldn't, I sent them to the next town or after Joseph set up practice, to him for more help. But I never needed to send anybody on for help with the burns. I had the gift.''

"I know.''

"That's right. I did it for you, too, didn't I?" She looked away from me out the window, but I knew she wasn't seeing the buildings and trees outside. She was seeing somewhere in the past.

"Annie was barely five, a little bit of a thing, but sweet in a big-eyed timid sort of way. I knew her from church. Her mother brought her.''

"Church?''

"Oh yes, I wasn't such a hermit then. Those were different times.''

"What happened?''

"As I said, Annie was badly burned. Her father said she'd pulled a kettle of hot water off the stove on herself. I had no reason not to believe him." She paused a moment before she continued. "The child was screaming, beside herself with the pain, and I was glad I was able to take the fire out of her burn and give her relief from the pain.''

Miss Eleanore's eyes came back to me. "She seemed better. She stopped crying. The burn was no longer hot, and the red was fading. And I was proud. I didn't see any reason to send her to Joseph. He might handle broken bones better than I could, but I could handle burns. It was my gift.''

She sank back into her pillow and shut her eyes again. I waited for her to go on, but she said no more. Finally I asked, "What happened?''

"She died that night.''

Chapter Eleven

In the silence that followed her words, little Annie seemed to creep out of the corner of the room where she'd been hiding. Only now I could see her better than I'd ever seen her before. I saw how tiny she was, much smaller than Chuck, and I could see her dark eyes, wide and frightened, on me. I wondered if Miss Eleanore would be able to see the little girl standing there beside me when she opened her eyes.

The door pushed open, and a nurse came sweeping in. I jumped off the bed as though I'd been stung.

Miss Eleanore caught my hand and held to it.

The nurse stared at me. "Are you supposed to have visitors, Miss Nellie?"

"Do you want me to leave?" I looked at the nurse instead of Miss Eleanore.

"No," Miss Eleanore said firmly. "Miss Busy-nurse is the one who is going to leave. Barging in, bothering a body when a body doesn't want or need to be bothered."

"Now Miss Nellie, you know we have to check your blood pressure every hour. Dr. Shelley explained all that to you just yesterday."

"Then get it done with and get out of here," Miss Eleanore said crossly.

The nurse wrapped the blood pressure cuff around Miss Eleanore's arm gingerly, as though she half expected Miss Eleanore to smack her hands. After she took the reading, she counted Miss Eleanore's pulse. A frown wrinkled her forehead as she wrote the numbers down on a pad in her pocket.

The nurse looked at Miss Eleanore and said, "I think your visitor should leave now. Dr. Shelley says you shouldn't get excited."

Miss Eleanore's grip on my hand grew tighter. "I'll say when I should get excited and when I shouldn't. Now get out of here."

The nurse's eyes slid away from Miss Eleanore to land on me.

"I'll leave," I said timidly.

"If you leave, Virginia Mae, I'm getting out of this bed and going with you. We'll just walk on home, and then we can finish our talk without all these interruptions."

The nurse put her hand on Miss Eleanore's arm. "Now you know you can't leave, Miss Nellie."

Miss Eleanore jerked her arm away from the nurse. "Why not? Are you going to tie me down again?"

"We hope you won't make us do that."

"Not if you'll get out of here and leave me alone."

The nurse took one last look at me before she left. My heart was beating fast, and I didn't know what to do. After the door swung shut behind the nurse's white uniform, I said, "Maybe I should go, Miss Eleanore. I can come back again tomorrow."

"No, no. You stay. I just need a minute to marshal my wits."

I looked from her to the door, half expecting the nurse to return with reinforcements to bodily throw me out of the room. I thought it might be wiser to slip away before that could happen, but Miss Eleanore still gripped my hand. I looked back at her small, wrinkled face that was almost whiter than the pillowcase, and suddenly I knew I'd stay till she was finished talking or the nurses forced me to leave, whichever came first.

"Now, where were we?" Miss Eleanore asked.

"You were talking about little Annie. You said she died, but it couldn't have been because of the burn. You healed that."

"Oh yes. Now I remember. No, it wasn't the burn. She had a head injury. I should have seen it when I looked at her. It must have shown in her eyes, her breathing, some way, but no, I saw only the burn. And because I didn't make her father take her on to the doctor, she died.''

"Nobody could blame you for that," I said.

"I blamed myself. I should have seen." Her voice was low, barely a whisper. "And the father blamed me."

"Why?"

"To keep others from blaming him. He abused the child. I realized that later when I remembered the bruises. He must have knocked her into the stove, causing the water to spill on her. The child was to blame for none of it."

The little ghost that was Annie faded away in front of my eyes. "Neither were you. I knew that all along."

Miss Eleanore smiled her odd, one-sided smile. "I didn't tell you all this so you'd like me, but so you'd understand the danger of the gift. I was so proud of my power to heal I let it blind me, and because of that pride, Annie died. I don't want that to happen to you."

"To me?"

"Of course, you. Providence sent you to take the gift from me, Virginia Mae."

"I don't understand."

Miss Eleanore began explaining patiently. "You see after little Annie, I was afraid. Afraid the same thing might happen again. So I thought it better if no one came to me for doctoring anymore. I closed myself away from the world. It wasn't hard after I heard what they were saying about me. Oh, the stories they told.

People who'd known me for years. People I'd taken care of."

"They should have known it wasn't your fault," I said, hardly able to bear the sadness on her face.

"I suppose they were frightened. I think perhaps they had always been frightened of my gifts but I'd just never noticed it before. Anyway, after that I sent those still brave enough to come to me on to young Dr. Joseph."

"Even with burns?"

"I took the fire out of the burns first, but after all the stories about little Annie, few came anymore. While that was what I wanted, still the gift is one of good, and I never thought when I decided to have nothing more to do with people that I'd end up having no one to pass the gift on to when the time came."

"You could give it to Dr. Shelley."

She snorted. "Young Dr. Joseph? He laughs at my cures. No, Providence sent you to me, Virginia Mae, and we can't fight Providence."

"You want to give me the gift?" My heart jumped strangely in my chest.

"Yes." She was watching me closely.

I backed up a step or two from the bed. "I couldn't."

"The gift just needs a vessel. You would be that vessel."

I remembered Chuck's wide eyes on me as he talked about me being a witch, and how Mark had looked at me as though he wasn't too sure I wasn't. "I can't," I said again.

She looked at me for another long minute before she turned her eyes to the window. A tear trickled out of her good eye and down her cheek. "There is no one else, Virginia Mae. No one else."

I stared at her and thought of myself, alone and shut away from the world. I'd always been different, but this went beyond different. "I'm scared," I said at last.

She turned to me slowly. "And so was I when Grandfather gave me the gift, and a little excited as well. Of course I was older." She studied me thoughtfully with a look of doubt. "You are young for the burden. Perhaps it would be better to let it die with me. Not many trust the old cures anymore, anyway."

She looked so tired and disappointed that I made myself smile and say, "But what about Providence?"

Her face brightened. "Then if you're willing, my child, lean close. First you must know the rules."

As she began reciting the rules, I wondered if I'd be able to remember them all. I couldn't tell anybody that she had given me the power. I couldn't refuse to help anyone who came to me with a burn nor could I take money for the healing. I couldn't reveal to anybody the secret of the power, for if I did I would lose it just as she was losing it by telling me now. I should take great pains to pass the gift along before I died to someone who would use it wisely. Oddest of all, I could tell no one I had this power to take the fire out of a burn.

"But how would anyone ever know to come to me?" I asked.

"Providence will bring you the first people you must help, and then others will tell." Her voice was weaker, and her face was pale. "Now listen carefully while I tell you the secret. All these years I've held it close inside me, but now it's burning to get out and into your ears."

I listened, hardly understanding anything she said. When she was through, I knew there would be no way that I could ever remember the strange words she had whispered to me. So the gift would die with her, after all.

Miss Eleanore must have seen the confusion on my face because she smiled and said, "You understand more than you think you did, Virginia Mae. The gift buries itself deeply in your mind. It will surface when it's needed."

"Is that all then?" I asked, wondering if I should thank her, or what.

"That's all, and now I can truly rest." She lay back with a deep satisfied sigh. "I was so afraid you weren't going to come in time."

"I would have come sooner but Dr. Shelley didn't want me to." I knew that wasn't exactly the truth as soon as I'd said it. I'd been afraid to see Miss Eleanore so sick.

"Joseph doesn't know as much as he lets on. Fancy thinking this place is a better place for me than my rocking chair at home with my dearies close by." She grabbed my hand again. "You will take care of the dearies, won't you, Virginia Mae?"

"Of course I will. Until you can take care of them again yourself."

"You are a gift, Virginia Mae. The nicest gift Providence ever sent me."

I leaned over and kissed her forehead.

"Now I think I'll sleep for a while, child." She closed her eyes, and her grasp on my hand relaxed.

When I looked up, Dr. Shelley was standing in the door. I didn't know how long he'd been watching, but he was frowning and I felt a sinking feeling inside me.

"I'm leaving," I said quickly, ducking my eyes away from his and wishing I could somehow get out the door without having to pass close to him.

He let me pass and then followed me out into the corridor. I wanted to run for the elevator, but instead I stared at the blue carpet and waited for whatever he was going to say.

"Your mother's waiting for you downstairs in the lobby," he said.

I dared a look up at his face. He was still frowning, but it wasn't exactly an angry frown. He looked more like he was puzzled or maybe even embarrassed.

"I'm sorry, Dr. Shelley, but I had to come see Miss Eleanore."

He put his hand on my shoulder. "It's all right, Ginny. I just didn't understand before, but I do now."

"Can't you let her go home? I'd stay with her."

He shook his head slowly. "She's too sick, Ginny. She needs to be here."

When I turned toward the elevator, he said, "You can come back to visit her again tomorrow, Ginny, but next time don't stay so long. Okay?"

I looked back at him. "Okay."

Mama met me at the elevator downstairs. "Did Dr. Shelley see you?"

"Yes, but it's all right. He says I can come back to see Miss Eleanore tomorrow."

"That's quite a change from what he said down here. What happened?"

"I'm not sure."

"Well, whatever it was, we'll just be glad of it. The old lady did seem especially happy to see you." Mama smiled and looked at her watch. "It's not too late. What say we go up and look at the new babies before we leave?"

The plastic bassinets on wheels were all lined up in front of the nursery viewing window. I felt silly staring at babies I didn't even know, but Mama was smiling, admiring them all. When the nurse on the other side of the window motioned at us and lifted her eyebrows in question, Mama pointed to one of the babies. The nurse picked up the baby, pink blanket and all, and brought it close to the window so we could see it better. The baby's face was red, and as we watched, it began to cry.

"Isn't she sweet?" Mama asked, a soft silly look on her face.

I didn't say anything till we were back downstairs headed for the car. "Why did you pick that baby?" I asked.

"The nurse thought one of them belonged to us, and that baby looked like you when you were born."

"I wasn't very pretty, was I?"

"I thought you were beautiful."

I looked over at her to see if she was kidding, but there was a dreamy look on her face. I said, "Do you think Cathy will have a boy or a girl?"

"I don't know."

"They want a boy, don't they?"

"I think maybe Jerry's said that, but it doesn't really matter with the first one."

"How about with the fourth?" I asked softly.

Mama put her arm around my shoulders and hugged me. "You've worried more about not being a boy than your daddy and I ever worried about it, Ginny. We liked you the way you were when you were a baby, and we like you the way you are now."

"But I'm different from the others."

"Not so much. Everybody feels a little different when they're thirteen. It's part of growing up."

"Do you think Miss Eleanore felt different when she was thirteen?"

"I think she probably did," Mama said as she got in the car. "I know I did."

"But she's still different. People think she's strange." I stared straight ahead out the windshield. "Chuck thinks she's a witch."

"Chuck watches too much television."

"I know she's not a witch, but she is different from most other people."

"But that's one of the reasons you like her, isn't it, Ginny? Because she is different."

"But I don't want to grow old and live by myself and have people think I'm a witch."

Mama laughed. "Now why would they do that?" But when I didn't laugh or smile, she became serious again. "Things happened to Miss Nellie to make her the way she is."

"She says it was Providence."

"Maybe it was, but even so, the same things won't happen to you. I don't think you have a worry in the world of becoming a hermit when you get old. You've got too much family for that."

I didn't say any more, but I thought of the gift Miss Eleanore had given me. That same gift had made her shut away the world. It might do the same thing to me.

I tried to remember the words she'd whispered to me. I could only think of two or three, and they were so strange I wasn't sure I'd remembered right. I'd never be able to use the gift no matter what Miss Eleanore had said about me understanding more than I thought I had. Maybe when I went back tomorrow I should tell her the gift was wasted on me. Still, she'd looked so glad after the telling of it. What did it matter whether I ever used it or not?

With that thought, I felt better. I leaned back in the seat, shut my eyes, and wondered if Mark would want to go with me tomorrow when I went over to Miss Eleanore's house to turn Hawk loose.

Chapter Twelve

Mama came up to my room early the next morning. "Jerry called a while ago. He's at the hospital with Cathy."

I woke up at once. "Has she had the baby?"

"Not yet. It usually takes a while with the first baby." Mama looked excited, but nervous. She was wearing her going-to-town clothes. "As soon as your father is through milking, we're going over to Millersburg."

"You want me to get dressed to go, too?"

"No, I think it'd be better if you and Chuck stayed here. It might be a long day. But Cynthie is dying to go, and I told her she could if you didn't mind staying at home with Chuck."

"I don't mind." I sat up. Light was just breaking outside.

"Charlotte spent the night with Sara. You can call her to come home as soon as you think they might be up. Say around eight or nine. I'd make Cynthie stay with you, but she wants to be there with Cathy so much."

"I can take care of Chuck."

"I know you can." Mama stopped at the door and added, "Be careful with the fire."

"I fixed Miss Eleanore's fire all the time."

"That doesn't mean you don't need to be careful," Mama said. "Daddy will be home in time to milk if we're not home before that."

Too excited to go back to sleep, I got up and went down to the kitchen.

"You'll be okay?" Mama asked as she put her coat on. Daddy and Cynthie were already in the car waiting for her.

"I take care of Chuck all the time."

"Usually there's somebody else around, but I guess you are thirteen now. I put the number of the Millersburg hospital by the phone if you need us for anything," Mama said and was out the door without another glance back. Her mind was already on Cathy.

When Chuck got up, I told him about Cathy while I fixed his cereal.

"You mean we're here by ourselves?" Chuck asked.

"Yeah. Are you scared being here alone with a witch?"

Chuck looked like he wanted to throw something at me, but then he just dug his spoon into his cereal. "You might not be a witch, but you are mean."

Chuck's hurt, wary look was familiar, and I was ashamed when I realized I'd been teasing him just the way the sisters tease me. I sat down at the table across from him. "I'm sorry I said that, Chuck."

"Mama says it's because you're a teenager now. That you won't want to play with me so much anymore. That you'll have new things you'll want to do."

"Oh, I won't change that much. We'll still play ball and stuff, and I'll try extra hard not to tease you. Okay?"

He looked up at me and smiled. "Okay."

"Come on, now. Let's go see if we can find Spider-man on the television."

"Do you think Mark will come over?"

"Maybe."

I waited too late to call Charlotte at Sara's house. They'd already left for church. It didn't really matter since I didn't see how I could get to the hospital to see Miss Eleanore, anyway, unless Mama and Daddy got back early. Miss Eleanore would understand when I explained things Monday.

At lunchtime, we ate our hot dogs in the living room in front of the television, something Mama never let us do unless we were sick. The wind was blowing and it was cold outside, but I kept the fire burning so it was warm in the living room.

Chuck had just turned the television off after the last cartoon when he looked out the window and yelled, "Mark's coming."

He took off for the door, ducking behind the stove as always. I'd seen him do it a hundred times, and I'd heard Mama yell at him as many. I yelled, too, but not soon enough. He tripped and crashed into the stovepipe, knocking it loose from the back of the stove. Smoke and soot blew out into the room.

Jerking Chuck back, away from the stove, I ran for pot holders to put the hot pipe back in the stove. I could hear Chuck screaming, but I had to fix the stovepipe first before the house caught fire.

"What's wrong?" Mark asked from the door.

"Chuck fell into the stove," I said. The pipe scorched the pot holders, but I finally slipped it back into place.

My stomach rolled over when I looked at Chuck's face. His whole cheek was an ugly, purplish-red scorch. Chuck reached up to touch it, but I held his hand away.

"Do you want me to call Dad?" Mark asked.

"In a minute." I stared at Chuck's face while my insides started to shake. "We need to take him to Miss Eleanore."

Chuck started crying louder.

"She couldn't help him," Mark said.

"But she could. I know."

Mark looked at her. "Miss Eleanore died this morning. Dad sent me over to tell you so you wouldn't go to the hospital to see her."

"Died?" The room faded away from me while I saw the empty rocking chair with the two cats waiting. Chuck's screams brought me back.

"I'm sorry, Ginny," Mark was saying. "But she was so old and weak that Dad said it was a wonder she'd lived as long as she did after the stroke."

"She couldn't die till after she did the gifting," I said. Mark gave me a funny look, and Chuck's screams reached a new level. Picking Chuck up, I half led and half carried him to the couch. "Go get some ice, Mark, and a wet rag or something."

"I think I should call Dad."

"Okay, but get the ice first. We've got to do something to keep it from hurting so bad."

You can do something, a little voice inside me whispered, and I remembered Miss Eleanore's words. Providence would supply the first opportunities for me to use the gift. I looked down at Chuck's face, and my heart began thumping with fear. I couldn't do it.

If someone needs your help, you can't refuse, Miss Eleanore had said.

"Chuck," I said. "I'm going to try to help you."

Chuck stopped crying. "It hurts, Ginny."

"I know. But I may be able to make the hurt go away if you're brave enough to let me try."

His eyes were wide as he said, "The way you said Miss Nellie did for you?"

"Right. But you have to be brave because for a few seconds it's going to hurt even worse."

Chuck began crying again.

I held him close and kissed his forehead above the burn. Then I took a deep breath, touched my fingers to my lips and lightly traced them across the burn. From deep inside me the strange words bubbled up to my lips. Chuck screamed louder, but I paid no attention as the words spilled out of me till I was empty.

Silence rang in the room when Chuck stopped screaming. "It doesn't hurt anymore," he said.

"I know," I said. The skin still looked scorched, but the ugly red was fading away.

His eyes on me were bright and scared. I was scared, too. More now that I had taken the fire out of his burn than I had been before. I looked up to see Mark holding out the rag with the ice and staring at me.

"I had to do it," I said. "I couldn't let him keep hurting."

When he just kept staring at me, I took the wet rag from his hand and gently wiped Chuck's face. "You were very brave, Chuck."

Chuck grabbed me and hugged me. "If you're a witch, Ginny, you're a good witch, and I'm not afraid of you."

"I'm not a witch, just your big sister, and if you ever run behind that stove again, you'd better be afraid of me because I'm going to wallop you but good."

"I called my dad," Mark said. "He's on the way over here."

"That's okay," I said.

"What are we going to tell him happened to the burn?" Mark asked.

"I don't know. The truth, I guess," I said.

"He won't believe it. I'm not sure I do, and I saw you do it." Mark slowly reached out and touched Chuck's cheek. The skin was rough, funny looking, but the red was gone.

When Dr. Shelley got there, Mark met him at the door. "It wasn't as bad as we thought, Dad. We put some ice on it, and it's okay now."

Dr. Shelley pushed past him. "I'd better have a look at it, anyway, since I'm here."

He looked at Chuck's face for a long time. Then he glanced over at Mark before his eyes settled on me. "Mark, why don't you and Chuck go outside and take a walk or something? I want to talk to Ginny."

"Get your coat," I told Chuck as he started to follow Mark outside.

Dr. Shelley was silent for a moment after the door shut behind them. His eyes on me were sharp and intense. "It can be a burden," he said at last.

"I didn't want her to give it to me." Tears filled my eyes. "But she said there was no one else. Then afterward, after the gifting, I didn't think I'd ever remember enough of what she told me, to use it."

"But you did."

I remembered how the words had risen out of me without me even needing to think about them and then had fallen back deep inside me out of reach again. "It was scary."

"You didn't have to use it, Ginny."

"But then Chuck would still be hurting. It was a terrible burn, Dr. Shelley."

"I could have treated it."

"You couldn't have made it stop hurting."

Dr. Shelley stood up and paced across the room twice before stopping to stare down at me again. "Did she tell you about little Annie?"

"She told me. I knew all along that Miss Eleanore couldn't have killed anybody."

"But she did in a way by trying to doctor what she couldn't doctor."

I was trembling inside. "I'll try to give the gift to you if you want me to."

"No," he said after a moment. "Right or wrong, it's your burden now. Pray it's kinder to you than it was to Miss Nellie."

I walked out on the porch with Dr. Shelley when he left. Chuck was sitting on the steps by himself. "Where's Mark?" I asked.

"He said he had to go on home," Chuck said.

"Oh, I see." I looked across the field to the tree house, wondering if he'd stopped there. I wanted to run after him, but what could I say to him if I found him? He thought I was a witch.

"Come on." I tousled Chuck's hair. "Let's go in. Maybe Mama will call soon and tell us if we have a niece or a nephew."

"I hope it's a boy. I'm tired of being the only boy in the family."

Right after Charlotte came home, Mama, Daddy and Cynthie pulled in. Everybody was so excited about Cathy's new baby boy they didn't even notice the place on Chuck's face. Actually, although there was this funny-looking shadow lying across his cheek, it didn't look anything like a burn anymore. I slipped away before Mama could realize it wasn't just dirt.

I wanted to go over to Mark's house and ask him to go with me to turn Hawk loose like I'd planned. I hesitated under the tree house for a minute before I went on through the woods toward Miss Eleanore's house. Yesterday I could have asked him. Today I couldn't.

As I walked through Miss Eleanore's trees, I wished I could see Miss Eleanore just once more. I needed to tell her about the burn on Chuck's face because she was the only one who could really understand.

By the time I walked up on her porch and opened her door, the need to see her was a heavy knot of pain inside me. Sunlight didn't come greet me when I went through the door. He and the black cat were both sitting in the rocker watching me.

"She's gone, dearies," I said softly. "But don't worry, I promised her I'd take care of you."

The chair seemed to move slightly, and I could imagine Miss Eleanore there, stroking the cats and nodding while she said, "You see, dearies, Providence has taken care of us."

I fed Hawk before I put the black hood over his head. After putting on Miss Eleanore's heavy glove, I urged him over on my hand the way I'd seen her do once when she was checking his wing.

The cats watched from the rocking chair as I carried the hawk outside. Jumping down, Sunlight followed me.

Mark was on the porch. "What are you doing here?" I asked.

"I followed you."

The hawk was so heavy I could hardly hold my arm out steady. "Miss Eleanore told me to let Hawk go."

"I'm not trying to stop you." He stepped to the side. "Is it okay if I come with you?"

"I'm not going far." I glanced out at the small open space to the side of the house where the road ran through the trees. "He can fly away here as well as anywhere."

Hawk dug his talons into the glove as we went down the steps. Once in the middle of the road, I untied his fetters. "Well, Hawk, this is it," I said, pulling the hood off the bird's head.

Hawk looked around as if he wasn't sure what was happening. "Go," I said and threw up my arm.

He flapped his wings and lifted off my hand. Then he hung there a moment before he began rising up between the trees, higher and higher far above us in the sky, until his shape was no bigger than my hand. His whistle came down sharp and keen as he floated away out of our sight over the treetops.

When I looked away from the sky, Mark was watching me instead of the hawk.

"I won't be like Miss Eleanore," I said. "She didn't tell me how to take off warts, and I don't know anything about her herbs."

"Just burns."

"Just burns," I agreed. "But I may never have to do that again. I can't tell anybody about the gift, and when we move, there's no reason for anybody to ever find out about it."

"I don't want you to move."

My eyes came up to meet his and then quickly away to the ground where Sunlight was softly winding his body around my legs. "Daddy's a tenant farmer. We always move sooner or later."

"Then I hope it's later."

I looked up at his face again. "But aren't you afraid that I'm a witch?"

"Like Chuck said, if you're a witch, you're a good witch, and I like you." He reached for my hand. Miss Eleanore's glove was so thick and heavy, I could barely feel his grasp. He looked down at our hands and said, "How come you're always wearing gloves when we hold hands?"

A giggle bubbled up inside me. "I don't know."

He pulled the glove off and clasped my hand firmly. Inside me something broke free and soared as high as Hawk had moments before.

Mark tripped over the yellow cat as we headed back to the house. "What are you going to do about the cats?" he asked.

"Sunlight will go home with me, but I'll have to ask Midnight what he wants to do." I glanced over at Mark. "Does that sound too crazy?"

"After today, I'm not sure anything will ever sound too crazy again."

The black cat was still in the rocking chair. Gingerly I reached down to stroke the cat, and he didn't snarl and spit at me but endured my touch. "I've got to go home, Midnight. I want you to come with me."

He stood up and shook all over as if to rid himself of my petting. I pulled my hand back. "You can come if you want to. You know where I live."

The cat glared at me. "Maybe I should open some cat food and leave it here for him," I said.

"If you do, he'll never follow you home," Mark said.

"He probably won't anyway."

"He might if you don't feed him."

I studied the cat doubtfully. "I guess I can always come back to see about him tomorrow if I have to. He won't starve in one day."

I took one last look around the room. Miss Eleanore was everywhere I looked. When I closed the door behind me, I felt like I was leaving her behind as well as the black cat. But then I picked up Sunlight and carried him down the steps, and as his purr began rumbling against my hand, I knew I was taking away more than I was leaving behind.

As we walked through Miss Eleanore's woods, I told Mark about the trees and their names. Once or twice we laughed, and it seemed only right.

When we were on our side of the fence again, I looked back. "Do you think they'll say it's haunted now?"

"Probably, but maybe there are good ghosts just like there are good witches."

"I'm not a witch, good or bad," I said. "I'm just me."

"I know." He leaned over and kissed me lightly on the lips. "I'll see you tomorrow." His face was red as he turned away from me toward his house. After a few steps he broke into a jog.

Rubbing my cheek against Sunlight's head, I walked slowly toward home. I wondered what Mama would say when she saw the cat. I wondered if Chuck had told them about the burn yet. He would, of course, sooner or later. Would the sisters tease me about this strange gift I had? One thing for sure, they'd tease me unmercifully if they knew I'd just gotten my first kiss.

I was just going under the tree house when the black cat streaked in front of me. Then stopping, Midnight waited for me to catch up with him at the fence. "So you decided to come," I said. "Miss Eleanore would be glad. She'd say it was Providence. Just like the gifting was Providence."

Whatever it was, I wouldn't fight against it. The gift was there within me. I couldn't change that, but Miss Eleanore had assured me it was a gift of good. I'd remember that and believe it even when the strangeness of it scared me. And I'd remember Miss Eleanore always.

I let Sunlight down, and the two cats and I walked across the pasture together. At the house I could see Cynthie and Charlotte watching me from the window. All at once I hoped they'd tease me, because that would mean everything was back to normal. Or as normal as it could ever be after knowing Miss Eleanore.

* * * * *

Did you hear about the war on flab?

My flab! Well, my mom, who's a gorgeous movie star, decided she couldn't have a fatso for a daughter. So she tried all kinds of stuff. Do I need to tell you that NOTHING WORKED? I didn't get skinny, I just got mad. And when I get mad, watch out....

Bigger is Better

SHEILA SCHWARTZ

Coming from Crosswinds in October

BIGGER-1

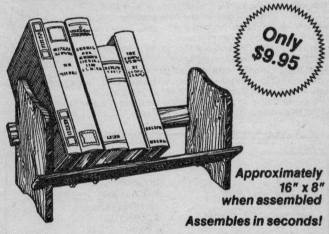